TRAPPED!

Slocum pushed the blond into the attic and followed quickly. His keen ears heard the pounding of feet up the stairs to the roof.

"They're out here," came the gruff voice. "I feel it in my bones. Mr. Crocker's offering a fifty dollar reward."

"And Mr. Thorvald's offered another hundred," shouted another.

Slocum struggled to lower the window without drawing attention to himself. He couldn't get the balky window closed. It was only a matter of time before they followed. He didn't want to shoot it out with them. . . .

"Here," Harriet called. "I've found the door back into the hotel—" Her voice trailed off. As Slocum looked past her, he saw why. Thorvald and another man with a Winchester rifle came up the stairs. They cut off any escape.

Slocum was caught between the men on the roof and Thorvald's squad of cut-throats . . .

OTHER BOOKS BY JAKE LOGAN

RIDE, SLOCUM, RIDE
GUNS OF SOUTH PASS
SLOCUM AND THE HATCHET MEN
BANDIT GOLD
SOUTH OF THE BORDER
DALLAS MADAM
TEXAS SHOWDOWN
SLOCUM IN DEADWOOD
SLOCUM'S WINNING HAND
SLOCUM AND THE GUN RUNNERS
SLOCUM'S PRIDE
SLOCUM'S CRIME
THE NEVADA SWINDLE
SLOCUM'S GOOD DEED
SLOCUM'S STAMPEDE
GUNPLAY AT HOBBS' HOLE
THE JOURNEY OF DEATH
SLOCUM AND THE AVENGING GUN
SLOCUM RIDES ALONE
THE SUNSHINE BASIN WAR
VIGILANTE JUSTICE
JAILBREAK MOON
SIX-GUN BRIDE
MESCALERO DAWN
DENVER GOLD
SLOCUM AND THE BOZEMAN TRAIL
SLOCUM AND THE HORSE THIEVES
SLOCUM AND THE NOOSE OF HELL
CHEYENNE BLOODBATH
SLOCUM AND THE SILVER RANCH FIGHT
THE BLACKMAIL EXPRESS
SLOCUM AND THE LONG WAGON TRAIN
SLOCUM AND THE DEADLY FEUD
RAWHIDE JUSTICE
SLOCUM AND THE INDIAN GHOST
SEVEN GRAVES TO LAREDO
SLOCUM AND THE ARIZONA COWBOYS
SIXGUN CEMETARY
SLOCUM'S DEADLY GAME
HIGH, WIDE, AND DEADLY
SLOCUM AND THE WILD STALLION CHASE
SLOCUM AND THE LAREDO SHOWDOWN
SLOCUM AND THE CLAIM JUMPERS
SLOCUM AND THE CHEROKEE MANHUNT
SIXGUNS AT SILVERADO
SLOCUM AND THE EL PASO BLOOD FEUD
SLOCUM AND THE BLOOD RAGE
SLOCUM AND THE CRACKER CREEK KILLERS
GUNFIGHTER'S GREED
SIXGUN LAW
SLOCUM AND THE ARIZONA KIDNAPPERS
SLOCUM AND THE HANGING TREE
SLOCUM AND THE ABILENE SWINDLE
BLOOD AT THE CROSSING
SLOCUM AND THE BUFFALO HUNTERS
SLOCUM AND THE PREACHER'S DAUGHTER
SLOCUM AND THE GUNFIGHTER'S RETURN
THE RAWHIDE BREED
GOLD FEVER
DEATH TRAP
SLOCUM AND THE CROOKED JUDGE

JAKE LOGAN

SLOCUM AND THE TONG WARRIORS

BERKLEY BOOKS, NEW YORK

SLOCUM AND THE TONG WARRIORS

A Berkley Book / published by arrangement with
the author

PRINTING HISTORY
Berkley edition/May 1989

ISBN: 0-425-11589-5

A BERKLEY BOOK ® TM 757,375
Berkley Books are published by The Berkley Publishing Group,
200 Madison Avenue, New York, NY 10016.

PRINTED IN THE UNITED STATES OF AMERICA

10 9 8 7 6 5 4 3 2 1

1

Fog held the San Francisco street in its murky grip, destroying visibility and muffling sounds from beyond a few yards. John Slocum walked carefully in the debris-littered alley. Every shadow held death for him. His fingers danced lightly over the butt of his Colt Navy slung in a soft leather cross-draw holster under his canvas duster. He shook all over and sent a cascade of trail dust floating to the mist-damp street. He wished this night was over. Waiting wore heavily on him, even if he showed more patience than the other three working their way across the street.

The gray mist blew away and gave him a better look at Portsmouth Square. Razor Vincent had gone home for the night and no longer stood on his small box shouting that the Celestials would kill all true Americans in their sleep. For this Slocum was happy. Vincent sharpened a razor constantly and often brandished it at passing Chinese. He missed often, and cut innocent bystanders of less Oriental heritage.

Soft sliding sounds—silk against silk—alerted Slocum that he wasn't alone. He forced himself into a doorway and drew his six-shooter. He was acting as lookout, and had to stop the Celestials rushing to aid Fah Lu in his opium den.

Slocum cursed his own stupidity for getting involved in such a harebrained scheme. Robbing an opium den was risky in a city like San Francisco. The Chinese controlled too much of the territory to make escape easy if anything went wrong. Slocum had wanted to rob a bank and ride hell-bent for leather into the woods to the north of the city on the other side of the bay. The local police force wouldn't chase far if it took them away from their precinct. They were poorly paid, and depended almost entirely on bribes and graft to make a living.

An opium merchant like Fah Lu had connections with a tong. The hatchet men might follow across the Rockies, across the Plains, across the Mississippi, across the world to recover their money.

Still, Slocum had seen the plan Josh Beaumont had sketched out, and it looked good. Beaumont and two others would break into the opium den. One Chinese guard stood just inside the door. His job was more to keep control inside the drug parlor than to prevent robbery. He would fall quickly.

While Beaumont held Fah Lu hostage, the other two would ransack the place. Beaumont thought as much as a thousand dollars might be kept on the premises. Slocum wondered how the man had come to this conclusion. More fog drifted into fingers and vanished, giving a clear view of the opium den's entrance just off Portsmouth Square.

The run-down building had seen better days than May of 1880—it hadn't even been new when the Celestials started pouring into San Francisco in large numbers in the 1850s and '60s.

Again came the soft and distinctive sound of rustling silk. Slocum peeked out around the doorway. Fog had lifted across the square, but he saw nothing.

He carefully cocked his Colt. He wanted to be ready when trouble came. And it would. He felt it.

Slocum fidgeted. Beaumont and the others had to be inside Fah Lu's opium den by now. He hadn't heard any commotion. That might mean everything was going according to plan. Or it might also mean everything had fallen apart.

Slocum stepped onto the sidewalk, head tipped toward Portsmouth Square to listen intently. Once more the sibilant, silken sound came to his ears. This time a new sound accompanied it. Slocum threw himself face-down in the street just as a heavy hatchet pinwheeled through the night and landed with a dull *thunk!* in the doorjamb behind him.

He rolled and rolled again, coming to his feet. His pistol sought a target, but he was alone in the square.

Slocum dropped flat as a knife slashed the air where his neck had been an instant before. He twisted around and fired at the Chinese killer looming behind him. The Celestial had simply appeared. Except for the faint noise made by the silk coat he wore, the man had walked the night like a ghost.

The sharp report filled Portsmouth Square with a rumbling echo. The Celestial's dying groans added to the racket. Slocum knew every tong member in San Francisco would be down on them in seconds.

He ran across the square and kicked in the flimsy wooden door leading down into Fah Lu's opium den. The cloying scent of the narcotic smoke filled his nostrils. Nose wrinkling at the odor, Slocum took the steps three at a time and landed heavily in the cellar. Bunk beds lined the walls. Opium eaters sat along one wall, heads lolling to one side and vacant expressions on their faces. The other wall held the smokers. Thick billows from water pipes and smaller hand-held pipes obscured them. Slocum knew they weren't in any better condition.

"Beaumont!" he called. It was stupid to call out a name during a heist. He knew it and didn't care. They had to leave. Now.

He swung around, staring back up the stairs. Three burly Celestials stood there, the dim light reflecting off hatchets and wicked, slightly curved knives. Slocum chanced a wild shot at them, more to drive them back than to kill them.

"Your friends have left," came a quiet voice. Slocum glanced over his shoulder. A tall Chinaman dressed in expensive silk robes stood in an alcove. Although not old, the Celestial had a long, thin white beard. "The robbery is at an end. The On Leong will not allow such an invasion to succeed."

"Fah Lu?" asked Slocum.

"You know me. That is good. One should always know the name of the man responsible for your death."

The three tong hatchet men rushed down the stairs. Slocum fired again, this time aiming carefully. One fell and blocked the way for the other two. He swung back to face Fah Lu. The Oriental had not moved away from the shadowy alcove—but he had vanished. It took Slocum a second to realize Fah Lu had pushed through a door in the side of the small depression in the wall.

The cellar was too thick with opium smoke for Slocum to breathe—or to think. He couldn't retreat. The On Leong tong men had the stairs blocked. Finding an escape in the rat-infested opium den was out of the question. They would have him in seconds.

Slocum rushed to the alcove and found the door Fah Lu had used. Slocum braced his back against one side and kicked hard. The door exploded into a well-appointed room. Slocum blasted through the door, six-shooter ready. He fired twice more and downed a hulking Celestial with a meat cleaver intent on parting his hair.

"Where're the others?" Slocum demanded of Fah Lu. He tried to remember how many rounds he had fired, but he couldn't be sure.

The tall Chinaman drew out one hand sporting impossibly long fingernails and pointed. The two gunmen who had accompanied Beaumont hung on meat hooks at the far side of the room.

"The other escaped with a considerable amount of money. That will not be permitted. His name is Beaumont?"

Slocum fired directly at Fah Lu. The first shot missed by inches. The hammer fell on an empty cylinder as he lined the Celestial up for a killing shot.

"Take him," Fah Lu said in a cold voice. "Torture him!" He switched to singsong Chinese. Slocum heard footsteps above and behind him. The entire building came alive, and he was the one they were hunting.

Where had Beaumont gone?

Slocum thrust his Colt Navy back into its holster. He pulled out the thick-bladed knife he always carried at the small of his back. Stabbing out, he cut one tong man trying to force his way through the narrow door leading back to the opium den. Slocum knew he could never go that way. His left fist traveled less than a foot and landed squarely in the Celestial's belly. The man doubled up. Slocum again found Lady Luck on his side. The gasping Chinaman blocked the way for those behind.

From the commotion inside the opium den, Slocum guessed a dozen other On Leong tong members had entered.

He rushed Fah Lu, knife flashing. The tall man sidestepped and made a small movement with his hand. Somehow, Slocum found himself cartwheeling through the air. He landed heavily on his back, the air almost knocked from his lungs. Through mist he saw Fah Lu bending over him.

Slocum lunged—and felt his knife sink deep into flesh. The Celestial howled in rage and pain.

Getting to his feet, Slocum sucked in a painful breath. It was enough to keep him going. His lucky attack had wounded Fah Lu. The man sat with his back against a wall, a long-fingernailed hand clutching at the flowing wound in his right shoulder. Slocum decided against trying to use the opium dealer as a hostage. Fah Lu might be protected by the tong, but that didn't mean he belonged to the On Leong. The hatchet men might kill him just to save face.

The stairs afforded his only hope for escape. Slocum raced to the head of the stairs, then slipped the bar holding the door shut. Stepping back, he let four more Chinamen rush down into the basement. Slocum remembered what had happened to the other two men who had tried robbing the opium den and had been caught. He wasn't going to be the third dangling from a meat hook.

He ran like hell.

Slocum found himself in an empty office building. If he had entered these halls during the day, he would never have thought Fah Lu kept his opium den below.

Crashing through a glass-fronted door, he fell into the street. The fog had returned. Before, he had cursed it as a nuisance that hid possible danger from his keen eyes. Now he thanked it. He could melt into the damp grayness and never be seen again.

He blundered around Portsmouth Square until he found a side street and took it. He didn't care where he went as long as it was away from Fah Lu and the Celestials so eager to split his head open with their deadly hatchets. Slowing, he sucked in the cold night air and tried to calm himself. His heart still raced.

He walked for ten minutes and then found an abandoned building. He slipped into the burned-out husk and knelt. It took him almost five minutes to reload. His hands still shook from the nearness to death. The image of the two men hung like sides of beef would haunt him for some time.

As he pushed the vivid image of their corpses from his mind, another thought surfaced. Fah Lu had said that

Beaumont had escaped with the money. How? The answer to that turned Slocum cold with fury. Beaumont hadn't intended anyone to escape—except himself. He had arranged for the other two to be killed. He had also meant for Slocum to die.

The On Leong tong was careful about randomly killing San Francisco citizens. They existed because the police could do nothing about them. Indeed, the police tolerated the tong because they kept the large Chinese population in line. Payoffs greased the ways too, Slocum knew. The huge profits from the opium dens found its way, in part, into greedy politicians' pockets.

But the hatchet man who had almost killed him would not have tried unless he had been alerted.

Beaumont.

Slocum knew he might be wrong. Word might have leaked to Fah Lu about the attempted robbery. The tong's sentries might have been better than either Beaumont or Slocum realized. That still didn't explain how Beaumont had fled with the money.

Either Beaumont had tried to do in his cohorts or had fallen victim to the tong's alertness. It didn't much matter to Slocum. Beaumont had money that was rightfully his.

Sliding his six-shooter back into its holster, Slocum returned to the street. Again the fickle fog had lifted. Slocum went cold inside when he saw where his random flight had taken him. He stood in the middle of Dupont Gai, the main street through Chinatown. Trying not to appear apprehensive, he crossed the street and walked close to the buildings.

Even though he saw no one, he felt eyes on him. Hundreds of eyes. How long would it be until the tong found him?

He cut up a cross street, going past dingy alleys filled with garbage and entrances to other opium dens. He turned down another street, angling for the docks. If he reached the Barbary Coast area, he could get into a brightly lit saloon and stay there until dawn. He stood a better chance of living to see another sunset if he got away from the heart of Chinatown.

He knew he was in for a world of trouble when he saw a line of men cross the street in front of him. They stood with arms folded. Thrust into broad silk sashes were the emblems of their trade: hatchets. These were tong assassins. And they had come for him.

Slocum glanced over his shoulder and saw furtive movement in the shadows of the alleyways. Trying to dodge down any of them was suicidal. The tall brick walls narrowed his chances for escape. He didn't even look behind. The tong members were out in strength. They would expect him to turn tail and run.

John Slocum had survived the War Between the States by doing the unexpected. When patience didn't prove enough, courage always did. He realized that a frontal assault was the last thing the Celestials expected.

He drew his Colt and fired at the tong member at the right end of the line. The man grunted and fell dead. Slocum rushed the line before they recovered from the shock of his attack.

A second and a third shot took out another Chinaman. His knife slashed through thick cotton and found a brawny arm. Blood geysered outward. Slocum kicked and sent the hatchet man to the street. Another shot opened a dark hole between the eyes of still another On Leong killer.

They milled in disarray, unsure of themselves. Slocum didn't stay to fight. He heard the heavy pounding of feet coming down the street from behind.

He added his own boots to the din from the running. All the demons of hell followed him—but he finally evaded them. Panting, he stopped just inside the swinging doors of the Cobweb Palace Saloon, out on a pier. A loud squawk and a string of curses caused him to yank his six-shooter out and point it at a brightly colored parrot flapping around the smoky, cobweb-festooned room.

"Don't go killing the parrot, mister," came a gravelly voice. "The owner's Abe Warner, and he don't take kindly to people threatenin' his bird. Go on, belly up to the bar and have a drink. You might make amends by giving the bird one, too. Old Warner Grandfather is right partial to French brandy."

Slocum snorted. Any liquor served in this place had never seen France. Cobwebs hung everywhere, turning the saloon into a firetrap. Pictures of nudes were barely visible through the dangling strands. The raucous parrot berated him and everyone else in the vilest terms imaginable.

"Who taught the parrot to cuss like that?" Slocum asked.

"Can't rightly say," the barkeep said. "The boss got him from a sailor. Reckon the salt taught Warner Grandfather all he knows. He never learned words like that around here. Cusses a blue streak in four, maybe five languages. Even Chinee. Leastwise, it sounds like he's swearing when he talks like them." The bartender ran down. Slocum realized this was a standard speech. Probably everyone commented on the bird and its foul language.

"Whiskey. Not trade whiskey, either," he said.

"Got some fine French brandy. Old Sawtooth back there was right. The bird does take kindly to people buying him a shot."

Slocum gestured for the barkeep to set the bird up with a drink. It fascinated him watching the green and blue parrot land on the bar and waddle over. The powerful serrated beak snapped hard on the rim of the shot glass and lifted it.

In an incredible display of agility, the parrot downed the amber fluid without spilling a drop.

"Now watch. This is the best part," said the barkeep.

The parrot tried to fly. The potent liquor had adversely affected the bird's ability to stay aloft. It wobbled and careened wildly, running into cobwebs and squawking incoherently. The barkeep laughed, as did the sailor who had first spoken to Slocum, and the few others in the saloon.

Slocum downed his own liquor, seeing that it had come out of the same bottle. Too many of the dockside saloons got money from crimp crews, gangs that came through to shanghai unsuspecting patrons. A knockout drink or a sock filled with sand and the incautious patron ended up with a sore skull on the way to Singapore.

"You look the worse for it," the barkeep said.

Slocum shrugged. He was alive. That made it a successful night for him.

"You're not in any kind of trouble, are you?"

"Who isn't?" asked Slocum.

"I mean trouble with the tong. The cops we pay off. The tongs we have more trouble with. They're just as likely to kill us as whoever they want."

"Why ask?" Slocum moved so that his hand rested closer to his cross-draw holster and the pistol weighing it down. He had never liked nosy bartenders.

"Nothing, mister. Don't go gettin' hostile on me. I just seen a chink poking his nose through the door and thought . . ."

Slocum's green eyes shot up to the dirty mirror behind the bar. He saw no one reflected there.

"Don't think," he said, nursing his shot of amber fluid. He couldn't call it whiskey, and it sure as hell wasn't French brandy. Whatever it was, it carried a kick that warmed his belly and returned life to his body. He had been through too much tonight. All he wanted to do was get his share of the take from Beaumont and get out of San Francisco.

"Don't get riled. It's just that you're the second man through here tonight that's got the look of a fight about him—a fight with the tong." The barkeep pointed to Slocum's duster. The heavy canvas had been cut in several places by sharp edges. He hadn't noticed it before, but he was bleeding from a shallow cut. "I see enough men with hatchet marks on them. They don't last long."

"The second man tonight?" asked Slocum, trying not to show his excitement at being on Beaumont's trail so quickly—and by sheer luck. "Who was the first?"

"We don't ask names in the Cobweb Palace. Nobody in San Francisco asks names."

"About my height, muddy brown eyes, brown hair? A scar on his cheek running from here to here?" Slocum traced out a path on his left cheek to show where Beaumont's scar was. The barkeep didn't have to answer. Slocum saw it in his eyes, the way they darted around, the sneaky look that came over the man.

"Could be. Don't pay *that* much attention to customers," he lied.

Slocum had five dollars in scrip in his pocket. He fished it out and made a point of straightening out the wrinkles. "That bird gets powerful thirsty, doesn't he? I like birds. I might be tempted to leave this for him."

"What would it take for you to do this charitable thing?" asked the barkeep, knowing full well what was expected.

"My friend, the one with the big package—"

"The canvas bag?"

"The canvas bag," Slocum went on smoothly. He knew Beaumont had put Fah Lu's money in something. He hadn't known it was a canvas bag until the barkeep told him. "Where might I find my friend?"

The barkeep's eyes fixed on the greenbacks. They weren't worth much, not when saloons printed and used their own trade dollars for most transactions. But the bills were more than the barkeep was likely to get otherwise.

"Never seen him before tonight. Don't know who he was." The barkeep licked his lips. "Heard him say he was going over to the Slaughterhouse for a drink or two. Maybe he likes the women there. Most of them are pigs. I prefer the whores at the Constitution, myself."

"The Slaughterhouse?"

"Down Kearney Street near California," the barkeep said. "Not more'n a mile."

Slocum spun and left the saloon, the greenbacks staying on the bar. He knew they had vanished from sight before he had gone through the swinging doors. He also knew the barkeep wasn't an honest crook—he didn't stay bought. Slocum had betrayed himself when he responded to the jibe about the tong.

The barkeep would be talking to an On Leong member before Slocum reached the end of the street. All he could hope was that the man hadn't lied about Beaumont going to the Slaughterhouse Saloon.

Slocum wanted his cut of the money stolen from the opium den. At the moment, he didn't much care what it took to get it.

2

John Slocum stepped out of the Cobweb Palace Saloon and stared up and down the street. The dawn turned the horizon a pearly gray. Pink light threatened to come roaring up and over San Francisco Bay and give brightness to the tawdry sights along the docks. Slocum walked to the side of the saloon along a dock and stared at the pilings holding up the main body of the saloon. A few small rowboats underneath the saloon banged and creaked against the wooden pier. He wondered if trapdoors opened into the back room to afford easy coming and going for crimps. A few indiscreet drinks might be all it took to end up on a ship bound for the Orient.

The crimps might not even be that subtle. A loaded-shot blackjack alongside the head served the same purpose and worked a damned sight faster.

The activity of crimps wasn't what interested him, though. He hunkered down and waited. Less than five minutes passed before the barkeep went out on a small platform at the rear of the saloon and waved. Two pieces of shadow from under the pilings broke off and quickly moved up a rope ladder.

Slocum's hand went to his Colt Navy. He stopped himself. At this distance he couldn't possibly hit either the tong killers or the treacherous barkeep.

The trio spoke quietly for several minutes. The barkeep took something—Slocum didn't doubt that the man had been paid off—and returned to the saloon. The two Celestials drifted as if they had traded feet for wheels. They made their way around the edge of the dock and started down the street, passing less than ten feet from where he crouched.

Slocum followed at a safe distance. He could remove the pair easily, but he had no idea how much ruckus he might cause doing it or how many other Chinese might come to their aid.

The tong men vanished when Slocum turned up Columbus Avenue. He paused, thinking they had laid a trap for him. After waiting fully ten minutes, he decided they had given him the slip. He frowned, worrying about his neck. Was the money Beaumont stole from the opium den worth having his head separated from his torso?

It wasn't, but Slocum thought he could get his cut of the robbery money and still get away from San Francisco ahead of the On Leong tong. The heist had not seemed a good idea to him, but he wasn't simply going to give up the money now that it had been so successfully stolen. Better for Slocum to spend it than to let Fah Lu buy more opium for his hopheads.

He considered returning to the Cobweb Palace and finding out what the barkeep had told the two Chinamen. He might have sent them on a wild goose chase. Or he might have put them on Beaumont's trail. Fah Lu wasn't the kind to let such a daring theft go unpunished. The money might even be secondary to punishing anyone with the temerity to steal from him.

Slocum followed the shoreline of the bay until he came to the Slaughterhouse Saloon. Except for the name painted in flowing gilt letters and the weathered wood sign, this might have been the Cobweb Palace. When he looked inside he expected to see a parrot diving at customers and cadging drinks.

The interior was more ordinary for a San Francisco saloon. Green-felt-topped tables were scattered around the walls, mostly reserved for gambling. One held five sailors playing poker. Another had a trio working on a game of Spanish monte. A few drunks were passed out on the battered tables in the center of the saloon. From the look of them, they had spent the night sprawled on the stained wood.

Two scrawny whores stood at the end of the bar talking with a seedy bartender. The man's walrus mustache drooped and needed waxing. He took an occasional turn at it, but the result was less than sartorially perfect.

Slocum stepped in and just stood. He had the uneasy feeling that he was missing something important. He had looked the place over from outside to be sure he didn't walk into the center of a gang of tong killers. He saw only white faces. The Chinese left this saloon alone, from the look of it. For that, Slocum gave a sigh of relief. Finding Beaumont and getting his share of the money would be hard enough without fighting off a dozen hatchet men.

The uneasiness grew as he went to the bar. The two whores looked him over. They both liked what they saw. One licked her ruby-painted lips in what she thought was a seductive gesture. The other batted her eyelashes in his direction. He ignored them.

The barkeep came over and said, "I can get you a drink, mister, but the way both Emy and Claudia are acting, you'd do better spending a dollar with them than drinking my rotgut, even if I do make the best damned Pisco Punch in town."

This took Slocum aback. He had never heard a barkeep

suggest a whore over a drink. The two usually went hand in glove—a whore might get a likely prospect to buy cheap whiskey at prices ten times too high. This put Slocum even more on guard. The Slaughterhouse Saloon made its money off pursuits other than whiskey and women.

"A drink," he said. "Nothing more. Don't have the money for a woman right now."

"They've both had a slow night. Hate to send 'em home without some action."

"You offerin' them to me for *free*?" Slocum knew something was wrong now. Once back in the cribs, he'd never come out alive.

"Maybe not for free." The barkeep poured a drink. Slocum brought it to his lips and pretended to sip. Cheap whiskey often hid the bite of drugs. The barkeep said, "They might deal. We don't get many in here that look as good as you. Most are horny sailors turned to leather by the sea. That's what they told me, at any rate." The barkeep returned to the two whores and talked with them in a low voice.

The one who had been batting her eyelashes at him came over. For his taste, she was too skinny. At least she was the better looking of the two.

"You excite me, mister. I been standing around all night. I *need* a man." She reached out and rubbed along his crotch. His hand shot out and caught her thin wrist. He didn't like the idea of her hand drifting so close to his Colt Navy.

"I've hardly got enough money to pay for this drink," Slocum lied. He wanted to see her reaction. It told him he was being set up.

"That's all right," she said, shrugging off his plea of poverty "I *need* it. Christ, if I don't get it I go crazy." She rubbed up against him in a way she thought might persuade him to accompany her into the cribs. The front of her blouse opened and revealed a pair of meager paps. "If I don't do something, they're gonna trade me to the Bella Union down the street."

"So?" To Slocum one saloon and whorehouse was the same as another.

She shuddered. "They do awful things to a girl there. You got to drink with the customers. If you get too drunk, they sell you to *every*one with two bits. The others can watch for a dime. I don't want to end up like that. Help me, mister."

Her plea fell on deaf ears. Slocum looked past her to the barkeep and the other whore. They were paying more attention to what went on in the cribs than to the action in the saloon.

A man stood in the door leading to the rear of the saloon. His back was toward Slocum. When he turned, Slocum knew he had come to the right place. Beaumont held out a single greenback to another whore standing in shadow.

Slocum put his untasted whiskey onto the bar and tried to push past the woman. She clung to his arm with surprising strength.

"Don't go like this, mister. I'll do you for only a dime. A nickel! I need it, I tell you!"

The commotion caused Beaumont to look around. The greenback vanished from his hand as the whore he was speaking with bolted for the rear of the saloon. Beaumont saw Slocum and his mouth opened and closed like a beached fish. Of the canvas bag with the money from Fah Lu's opium den there was no sight.

"Beaumont!" Slocum called. "Stop, damn it!"

He shoved the woman aside roughly—and got knocked

to the floor. He struggled to get to his hands and knees as a gang of burly men rushed past him.

Crimps!

Slocum had seen enough of them working the saloons along the Embarcadero to know them by their trademarks. The socks filled with sand acted as blackjacks. Some carried iron bars wrapped in rags. Still others wore brass knuckles studded with vicious spikes. Nothing they used on their victims would kill outright. Warm bodies brought money from the captains of Orient-bound ships; they got nothing for dead men. In spite of this, Slocum knew they often tried to sell corpses to the masters of the ships. Collecting their crews, they often got too enthusiastic.

He got his feet under him and used the bar for support. As Slocum rose, he drew his pistol. The crimps made a beeline for Beaumont. Slocum couldn't let them take him, not without first finding out where he had hidden the money stolen from Fah Lu.

"Don't, mister," the whore begged. "They're killers. I don't want to see you get your head bashed in!"

"They're goddamned shanghaiers," he growled. He pushed past her and went to Beaumont's aid. The man had been unable to escape the crimps. Whatever trick he had used in Fah Lu's opium den hadn't worked here. Two of the men held his arms. He tried kicking, to no avail. They were overpoweringly strong.

Slocum shot one crimp in the side as his fist cocked for the blow that would rob Beaumont of his fight. The tall, red-haired shanghaier simply fell onto his back, not moving. Slocum saw the pink froth coming from the small bullet hole and knew he had shot the man through his lungs.

"He shot Billy!" one cried. The two remaining crimps stared at Slocum in disbelief.

"Let him go or you're fish bait," Slocum said, meaning

it. He brought up his pistol for the next killing shot.

Beaumont jerked free. Slocum cursed when he saw the man trying to run. He had to turn and trip him. If he hadn't, Beaumont would have vanished into San Francisco. Finding him again would have been well nigh impossible.

This gave the two crimps the chance to swing their blackjacks. One hit Beaumont on the side of the head, stunning him. The other barely missed Slocum's head—and it wasn't intended to stun. The huge bald-headed man had put his considerable strength behind the blow. They had seen their leader killed; they weren't likely to be gentle with him.

Slocum rode the force of the blow forward and away. He crashed hard into the floor. As he hit, his finger accidentally squeezed on his trigger. The report echoed through the now deserted saloon. He lay flat on his belly, the air knocked out of him.

From behind the long mahogany bar, Slocum saw the barkeep dragging out a scattergun. If he opened up with it, they'd all be dead meat. He struggled to get to his feet, but the strength had fled his body. He wasn't hurt bad. He just couldn't move until he got his lungs working again.

"Got him," the bald crimp gloated. "Let's take 'em both. We can use the money."

"A fine pair for Cap'n Mellick," the other said. "And we only got to split the money two ways."

"Billy woulda liked that," the bald one said, laughing harshly. They worked to get Beaumont into the rear of the saloon. Slocum blinked back tears and finally got his breath back. The barkeep had him covered with the sawed-off shotgun.

"Don't go gettin' any fancy ideas, mister. Emy and

Claudia told me they didn't want to see you blown all over the place."

The barrels looked big enough to crawl down. Slocum didn't move. His arm was trapped under him, the Colt Navy still in his grip. The bartender couldn't see that his victim had a drawn gun—not that it did Slocum much good.

He waited for his chance. It came when the crimps returned for him. For an instant, the barkeep's attention turned to them. Slocum surged and got to his knees. His six-shooter came up and fired. The slug took the barkeep high in the chest, rocking him back. The shotgun went off with an ear-splitting roar.

Slocum used the confusion caused by the barkeep's weapon to swing around on the crimps.

He fired point-blank into one. It didn't have any effect. He didn't know if he or the shanghaier was more startled.

Slocum knew he couldn't fight his way free. He kicked out, rolled, and kept rolling until he crashed hard against the saloon wall. Back against the wooden wall, he got to his feet, took another shot at the crimps, and ducked outside.

Cursing his bad luck, he made for the far side of the street. He had to reload—and find Beaumont before the shanghaiers spirited him away. Captain Mellick, one had said. That was Beaumont's fate. Slocum looked across San Francisco Bay and tried to guess which of the China clippers was commanded by Mellick. There were a full dozen of the sleek ships anchored and waiting for new crew members. Finding Beaumont once the crimps took him away from the saloon would be hard. Mellick's ship might even sail before Slocum could find out where the stolen money had been hidden.

Ready for battle again, Slocum circled the Slaughterhouse Saloon and slid down the steep embankment. He came to rest in ankle-deep mud and rotting fish. Making his way along the shore, he saw the ladder going up into the saloon. A trapdoor popped open and Beaumont was lowered using a block and tackle. The bald crimp followed on the rope ladder and dropped into the longboat. In the saloon, Slocum saw the other shanghaier working at the free end of the rope attached to the pulleys and Beaumont.

"Got 'im," called the bald-headed man. "Get your ass down here and let's be gone. This damn place is bad luck!"

"Billy won't argue that," the other said as he started down the rope ladder. "Nor will I. The bastard's bullet busted my goddamn knife. Snapped the blade off."

Slocum smiled grimly. That explained why he had failed to kill the man with his point-blank shot. He had unluckily hit the crimp's sheathed knife. That wouldn't happen again.

"We can come back for him. We still got to get three more for Mellick 'fore he sails."

The crimps unfastened the unconscious Beaumont from the rope and started to put out to sea. Slocum had other ideas.

He stepped into view and brought up his Colt Navy. From this range he couldn't miss. He was pissed and didn't mind if he shot both crimps down. What he wanted more than anything else, though, was a word with Beaumont. Slocum wasn't going through all this to lose the money stolen from Fah Lu.

"Beach your boat over here," he called. He cocked the hammer. The sound it made was a death peal, and both crimps knew it.

"We got no choice," one said to the other. The bald-headed man shrugged and put his back to the oars. The longboat crunched into the mud and sand not five feet from where Slocum stood.

"What now, mister?" asked the one sitting in the stern.

"Dump him onto the beach. Then you can go sell yourselves to Mellick, for all I care."

"He that good a friend of yours? Hell, mister, we'll cut you in. We're getting a hundred dollars a head. We'll give you thirty-five for him. He's got the look to him. He'd last the whole damned trip to Singapore."

"Dump him," Slocum said coldly.

The bald-headed crimp smiled crookedly. "It may not be that easy. We got a duty to do. There's ships expectin' us to deliver able-bodied seamen."

Slocum worried about his change in attitude. His eyes flashed from one man to the other, and he knew something had changed.

He ducked and tried to spin around. A numbing blow drove him to his knees. Stars came out, even though it was just past dawn. The pain spread through his head and shoulders and kept him from raising his pistol. Slocum tried to squeeze off a shot and failed.

The second blow sent him face-first into the bay. He felt the padded iron rod hit his head, then water closed around his face and he sank beneath the waves.

3

John Slocum tried to move. He couldn't. His arms and legs were securely bound. Forcing his eyes open proved painful. He stared straight up into the cloud-flecked blue sky above San Francisco Bay. From the way he was tossing up and down he knew he was in a boat.

"He's back with us," cackled the bald-headed crimp. The man used the toe of his huge boot to nudge Slocum in the ribs. "You got any last requests?"

"Go to hell," Slocum mumbled. The two shanghaiers just laughed at him.

He turned his head to one side and saw Beaumont. The man was still unconscious. From his pale, drawn face and the harsh, staccato breathing that sounded like a wounded locomotive, Slocum wondered if Beaumont would live long enough to be sold into slavery aboard an Orient-bound ship.

"What's wrong with him?"

"We might have hit him too hard," the bald man said. His tone told Slocum there was more.

"Shouldn't have let the chink use that knife on him like that," the man in the stern said. "He's losin' blood too fast. Not even Mellick will buy a dead man."

"Chink?" asked Slocum.

"Who do you think conked you on the head?" The bald

man laughed harshly, his confidence back. "One of the On Leong boys did it. They been dogging your tracks for some reason. They gave us both of you in return for talkin' a bit with this one." Baldy kicked Beaumont. The man didn't stir.

"A hatchet man?"

"He used the butt end of his hatchet on you. Damn, but he was good. Don't know how they teach those Chinee monkeys to use them axes. They ain't good for nothing else," opined the man in the stern.

Slocum closed his eyes and tried to force the nagging pain from his head. It didn't work. He shifted his weight and was rewarded with a boot to the ribs.

"Stay still. Don't go tippin' us over. There's sharks in these waters."

"And," cut in the other one, "the water stays cold the year round. You wouldn't last a minute trying to swim." He laughed. "Especially since we got you trussed up like a stray cow. You'd go straight to the bottom of the bay."

Slocum tried to take inventory, hoping they had missed his knife at the small of his back. They hadn't. His ebony-handled Colt Navy was missing, too. Even the two-shot derringer he carried in the top of his boot had been taken. The crimps knew their business. He was in for a long sea journey he didn't want to take.

Drowning in San Francisco Bay might be better.

Slocum pushed such nonsense from his head. Unlike most of the crimps' victims, he wasn't drugged or beaten unconscious. Beaumont could never escape on his own. Slocum could—and would.

The bald-headed shanghaier continued rowing with powerful strokes for another twenty minutes. The cold salt spray hit Slocum in the face and caused him to wince when it got in his eyes. He jerked when the longboat crunched into the side of a China clipper. A metal platform hung over the side, a rope ladder dangling under it. A half-dozen sailors scampered down the ladder to secure the longboat and get their two new crew members aboard.

"Where's the good captain?" called Baldy. "We got prime seamen for him."

"Captain Mellick's in the hold checking cargo," came a gravelly voice. "I'll take care of ye."

"Right you are, Mr. Woodward." Baldy said to the other crimp, "He's a harder case, that Mellick. Don't let 'im rook us, now."

Slocum was dragged up and onto the schooner's deck. He lay trussed and unable to move while the two crimps bargained with the first officer over him and Beaumont.

"Damaged goods," complained Woodward. "That's all we ever get from the likes of you."

"Billy's always given you prime seamen. Just like these two."

Woodward pushed back his sandy hair and cocked his head to one side. "Where *is* Billy? Why'd he send the pair of you to deliver the cargo this time?"

"He, uh, he got a bellyache."

"Mellick doesn't like dealing with anyone but Billy," Woodward said. "I'm not sure I do, either. Unless it's worth my while."

In spite of his predicament, Slocum was fascinated watching how the blond officer negotiated. Slocum guessed that the captain had already given his first officer the money for two new crewmen. If the first officer dickered a better deal, he kept the difference.

"We'll give the pair of them to you for two hundred," said Baldy. "That's a fair price, it is."

"It's robbery on the high seas!"

"Make it one-fifty, then. The one is in a bit of a drunk."

"He's losing blood by the bucket. He might not live long enough to clean up his own damned mess. One-twenty and not a cent more for the pair of them."

"The one's worth that on his own!" protested Baldy. He subsided and sullenly agreed to Woodward's price. The crimps took the money, squabbled over dividing it between them, then leaped over the railing and vanished. Slocum heard the oarlocks working and the gentle slapping of waves against the side of the longboat.

He was stranded on a ship bound for the Orient.

"Get them below. I don't want to see their ugly faces until we're a day at sea." Woodward spun and stalked off. Slocum saw the sly smile on the officer's face. He had bought two prime seamen for less than market price and felt pleased with himself.

Sailors roughly hauled Slocum and Beaumont to their feet. Sharp knives cut the ropes around their ankles, but no one removed the ropes around their wrists. Slocum stumbled along the slippery decks until the circulation returned.

"What's it worth to you to let me go?" he asked one sailor.

The seaman spat a red gob of betel nut and laughed harshly. "Mister, the captain would have my balls if he even thought I was going to let you go."

"How many of the crew have been shanghaied?" Slocum asked.

"More'n I want to think on," the sailor admitted. "Life's not that bad. Mellick's a hard man, but fair. Now take that mate of his. Woodward's scum. The worst kind. He enjoys bein' cruel just for the hell of it."

"Come with me. We can—" Slocum got no farther. The sailor shoved him into a tiny storage locker. Beaumont tumbled in behind, moaning in pain.

Slocum started to call out. The sailor slammed the small

door and barred it from the outside. Never had Slocum been so securely imprisoned. He wriggled around until he found a sharp hook on the wall holding tack. Rubbing the rope around his wrists on the point, he managed to get free in a few minutes. Circulation returned slowly to his hands, and he had bloodied himself.

He forgot about it as he knelt beside Beaumont. The man had turned even paler. Slocum dragged him to a spot where he could see the sky through a small iron grate overhead. This seemed to give the man strength enough to talk.

"Slocum?" he asked.

"Where's the money you took from Fah Lu?" Slocum had no time to waste. The sooner he found out what Beaumont had done with the money, the sooner he could get off this ship. He wasn't cut out to be a sailor. He preferred open spaces bounded by mountains where animals roamed. Most of all, he enjoyed being his own man. Life on a schooner meant living under someone else's orders. From what he had seen of Woodward and heard about Mellick, he wouldn't like obeying either man.

Beaumont stared at him, his brown eyes wide and unfocused. He tried to talk. Only incomprehensible croaks came out. Slocum shook him, then saw this was getting him nowhere.

"Do you want some water?"

Beaumont nodded. Through parched lips he said, "Ropes. Get 'em off, will you, Slocum?"

Slocum worked for several minutes getting the tightly knotted ropes free from Beaumont's wrists. The man sagged, making no effort to rub back circulation. Slocum saw blood slowly pooling under Beaumont. He rolled the man over and pulled up his coat.

During the war Slocum had seen men cut apart by minié balls and shrapnel. Every possible wound had been inflicted, and he had stared at them without a qualm. But the sight of Beaumont's back turned his stomach.

"Who did this?" he asked. Beaumont tried to answer and couldn't.

Slocum realized that he knew the answer and shouldn't have bothered asking. The same Celestial who had hit him with his hatchet had tortured Beaumont, trying to find where the money stolen from Fah Lu's opium den had been hidden. He heaved a deep sigh. His chances for getting his cut of the money had just vanished.

Beaumont must have told all. The flesh on his back had been cut into strips and pulled back. The pain alone would have loosened his lips.

Slocum sagged against the wood wall, his legs pulled up because of the tightness of the compartment. He had lost his chance at the money *and* had ended up a slave on a schooner bound across the Pacific. It might be years before he saw America again.

It might be never. Sailors didn't have long lives, especially those who had been shanghaied. All his skills were out of place aboard a ship. Who cared if he could ride all day and make a full hundred miles without killing his mount?

Slocum knew he'd survive. He was good at that. Ever since he had ridden with Quantrill's Raiders, he had survived well. Complaining about their bloody-handed butchery at Lawrenceville had gotten him gut-shot and left for dead.

He had lived. When he had returned to his home in Calhoun County, Georgia, he had found only an empty house. His parents had died during the war, as had his brother, Robert. Slocum had done what he could on the farm, turning it back into the showpiece of the county. A carpetbagger judge had taken a fancy to the farm and claimed that Slocum's father had neglected the taxes on the land during the war.

When the Reconstruction judge and his hired gunman had ridden in to take the farm away from Slocum, there hadn't been much fuss. Not as far as Slocum was concerned. He had buried the judge and his hired killer on the ridge near the springhouse. That same day he had packed a bedroll, saddled, and ridden away without a backward look. What he'd once had in Calhoun was gone. For years he had dodged the wanted posters for killing a federal judge. For years he had survived.

He would keep on surviving until he figured a way off this ship.

He wiggled his way to his feet and banged hard on the door. A voice on the other side growled. "Whatya want?"

"Water! This man's dying. He needs water."

"Let 'im die. Might be a better way to croak than lettin' that son of a buck Woodward have at 'im."

Slocum banged on the door again but got no response. Either the sailor posted outside had left or was ignoring him. Slocum didn't much care which. The result was the same.

He prowled the small closet of a room, hoping to find something he could use as a weapon. The rope on the hook—and the hook itself—were the best he could find. Hopping up, he grabbed the small iron grating over his head. He pulled himself up and peered out.

The ship was still in the bay. None of the sails had been unfurled yet, but the activity showed that the captain was preparing to leave before too long. Slocum guessed that the ship would leave on the evening tide. That gave him all day to work his way out of the rope locker.

Try as he might, he couldn't pry loose the walls or

floorboards. Every time he tried, he only bloodied his fingers more.

"Slocum?" came Beaumont's weak voice. Slocum didn't know how the man had clung to life this long. The sun had crossed overhead and was sinking into the west. From the activity on the ship's deck, he knew they would be sailing within an hour or two.

"What?"

"Didn't . . ."

"Speak louder," Slocum said, bending over and putting his ear close to Beaumont's mouth. "What did you say?"

"Didn't tell the Chinee anything. Not a word. Money's safe. Didn't know you were still alive. Sorry."

"Where is it?" Slocum resisted the urge to take Beaumont by the lapels and shake the answer from him. If the man hadn't revealed his hiding place when the tong's hatchet man had flayed him alive, a bit of shaking wasn't likely to get anything out of him.

"She knows."

"Who?" Slocum's mind raced. Beaumont spoke as if Slocum ought to know who he was talking about.

"Eleanore."

"Who's Eleanore?" Slocum sat back on his heels. He wasn't getting any more from Beaumont. The man gave a tiny gasp and died.

The ship began rocking from side to side as waves caught it. Slocum heard the anchor chains being pulled up. The ship was seeking the tide that would start it toward the Orient. And he didn't want to be aboard.

He had worked all day to pry loose a plank and had failed. He tried a different tactic now. Loud enough to be heard through the door, he said, "How'd you ever get that much money aboard? They searched me. You must have purt-near a hundred dollars, Beaumont."

He slipped a coil of rope off the hook and waited. In seconds the heavy iron bar slid away and the door flew open. The greedy sailor who had been posted as guard had come to relieve the incautious men of their money.

Slocum tossed the rope as if he were roping a stray. A quick jerk brought the sailor forward and onto his knees. It didn't matter that the seaman had a knife. Slocum kicked it out of his hand. A second twist of rope pinned the man's arms at his side. Slocum's fist drove all the fight from the sailor.

Slocum left him tied and gagged in the rope locker with Beaumont. It seemed fitting for the sailor to share a berth with a dead man. He retrieved the fallen knife and thrust it into his belt. It wasn't much, but it might give him the edge to escape.

Making his way to the deck, he saw the entire crew straining to lift the heavy canvas sails and catch the evening tide. Slocum raised his head up far enough to see that the ship had left San Francisco Bay—almost. On either side of the ship rose the steep, rocky cliffs that formed the Golden Gate. Another few minutes would see the schooner securely out to sea. If he didn't get away now, he was marooned on the ship for a long, long time.

Slocum heaved himself up and onto the deck. The rolling ship made walking difficult. Even worse, it drew attention. Of all the sailors on deck, only he had trouble with the wave-induced motion.

"Him!" shouted a sailor. "He's one of them we bought in Frisco. He got loose!"

Woodward turned from his vantage point amidship. The first officer's face clouded with anger when he saw the source of the commotion. "Don't stand there, fools!" he shouted. "Get him. Double rum ration to whoever brings him down."

Slocum lurched toward the railing. The sailor nearest him dashed to him and grabbed his arm. Slocum spun, flailing wildly. The attack had unbalanced him. It also sent the sailor reeling. Slocum got his feet back under him. He tried to time the up-and-down motion of the ship so he could face the dozen men forming a half circle around him.

"Take him alive," shouted Woodward. "I paid two hundred for him!"

Slocum knew the first officer was a liar. Woodward had given only a hundred and twenty for both him and Beaumont. Captain Mellick was more generous than any of the crimps had given him credit for. His first officer was the true crook.

When they came for him, Slocum used the motion of the ship to his advantage. He was catapulted forward by the rising ship. He dived, hit one man low, and bowled him over. The others tried to grab him but got in each other's way. Slocum had time to get to his feet and throw his arms around the large mainmast.

He looked up into the rigging. Men were swarming down to intercept him. The lure of double rum rations had proved a mighty incentive for them. Slocum knew he couldn't fight the men on deck. He started climbing. If it had been a tree, he would have little trouble.

The rope helped him as much as the rolling of the ship hindered. His gut churned from the motion, and he wanted to puke. Slocum held on and reached the lowest cross spar before the sailors above him climbed down to his level.

"I promise you the cat-o'-nine-tails if you let him get away," roared Woodward. The officer stood at the base of the mast and shook his fist at Slocum. The captain had left his post at the wheel and joined Woodward.

"You," Mellick shouted. "Get ye down here now! I will not have mutiny aboard my ship!"

Slocum edged along the spar out to the very end. He looked down at choppy green ocean. The San Francisco harbor had been gentle compared to this. Whitecaps formed as the heavy waves crashed against the side of the ship. He remembered what the crimps had said about sharks and the freezing cold. The salt spray in his face promised nothing but icy death.

He looked up from the ocean to the cliffs. The ship was passing through the Golden Gate. He had to act quickly or he would be trapped aboard for the rest of his life. From Woodward's expression, the man would beat him to death with the lead-tipped whip.

"Here, now, it ain't so bad," a sailor said, reaching out for Slocum.

Slocum snatched the stolen knife from his belt and cut the man's hand. He yelped and almost lost his footing on the rope-treaded spar. Slocum saw that fight was useless. A dozen sailors hung above him in the rigging. Others were coming up from below.

He looked again at the receding land, stuck the knife in his belt, and jumped.

He heard the angry cries from the ship. Then the schooner slid past him, captive of the waves and steady wind blowing to sea. Slocum shivered in the cold water and began swimming for land. He might die, but at least he'd die trying to get back to where he belonged.

The thought of all the money stolen from Fah Lu kept him going. And Eleanore, whoever she was, knew where to find it.

4

His teeth chattered uncontrollably. Slocum slapped himself. It didn't do any good. He pulled himself farther up onto the beach. In the distance male sea lions honked and growled at him from their rocky perch, their cries of outrage filling the night air.

Slocum stripped off his shirt and trousers, having long since discarded the canvas duster he had worn during the robbery. He wrung out the clothing and sat in his long johns, trying not to shiver even more. The cool wind blowing off the Pacific turned him cold all the way down his spine. He had no idea how long he had floated and kicked, stroked and struggled to get ashore. The schooner had sailed out of sight within minutes.

And he had fought for his life. Slocum hadn't been attacked by any sharks, but he had seen their shadowy fins cutting through the choppy water all around him as they hunted for dinner. Swimming directly for the lighthouse had saved his life. Without the beacon shining near the Sutro Mineral Baths he would have become disoriented in the dark and been washed out to sea.

"Damn," he said to himself as he shook the last drops of water from his lank black hair. "Nothing's gone right." Beaumont's death meant little to him. He had known the man for only a few days. Beaumont's obvious knowledge of the opium dens had convinced Slocum to take the chance at robbing Fah Lu.

Losing the money from the crime was bad. Having his ebony-handled Colt Navy stolen was even worse. He had a mate to it in his hotel room, but it would take long hours of work to find a suitable replacement and do the gunsmithing on it himself. He walked back to his hotel off Market, south of Portsmouth Square in the Mission District, trying to figure his best course of action.

Getting the hell out of San Francisco seemed the smartest thing he could do. The On Leong tong sought him. He had run afoul of crimps. If either the bald man or his partner saw Slocum again, they'd kill him on sight.

He should leave town immediately.

But the thought of Beaumont hiding the money kept bobbing to the surface of his thoughts and tantalizing him. Even more, the name Eleanore drew him. Eleanore knew where Beaumont had hidden the money. Who was Eleanore?

Slocum thought he knew.

Until he either found the stolen money or had convinced himself it was lost for good, he wasn't leaving. Slocum's stubborn streak always got him into trouble. It also kept him from finding life too dull. As he trooped through the hotel lobby and up the stairs, he knew he had a good chance of recovering the loot.

The tong thought he was shanghaied and on his way to the Orient. The hatchet man who had partially skinned Beaumont would have reported back to Fah Lu by now. They might still be searching for the money—or Fah Lu might have written it off as a loss and upped his opium prices to make up for it.

Either way, the tong killers weren't looking for him. If he showed some caution, the crimps would never see him.

He went about getting clean clothes put on, glad that he had an extra set. His spare Colt Navy took only a few minutes to oil and load. Slocum checked the loose floorboard and found the roll of greenbacks beneath it. He heaved a sigh of relief. He had accumulated almost a hundred dollars over the past few months. To have had it stolen too would have roused his considerable ire.

As it was, the lure of the money from the opium den robbery drew him powerfully.

He settled his six-shooter in his cross-draw holster and felt whole again. Although it was well nigh midnight, he decided he had to find the whore he had seen Beaumont talking to in the Slaughterhouse Saloon. She had to be Eleanore. Why else would Beaumont assume Slocum knew who he meant?

The trip across Portsmouth Square and along the Embarcadero made him jumpy. He couldn't help casting a cautious look in the direction of Fah Lu's opium den. He saw no activity outside. The Celestial might have closed down operations after the robbery. Finding a new cellar for his dope den wouldn't be hard, not in San Francisco.

Slocum considered going into the Cobweb Palace and finding the treacherous barkeep who had set the On Leong tong killers on his trail, but he decided against it. Finding the money and getting out of San Francisco was more important—and it meant he might live to enjoy the money.

The Slaughterhouse Saloon was crowded with sailors. The whores had no trouble keeping busy this night. Slocum studied the exterior of the wooden structure and saw where crimps had been at work earlier. Of the bald-headed man and his companion he saw no trace. Confident he wouldn't be recognized, he went into the smoke-filled saloon.

The saloon's tables were crowded with gamblers. Some wore fancy clothes. These professional gamblers lost a little and won a lot over the course of a night. The sailors they cheated seldom noticed or cared. Life at sea was harsh, and the sailors sought entertainment once they hit port. The gamblers provided a moment's thrill of winning before extracting their due.

"What'll it be?" asked a new barkeep.

"Where's . . ." Slocum let the name hang.

"The old bartender? He's gone. Didn't say where. The boss called me in to take his shift. We got good French brandy. Don't have too much nitric acid in it."

"Beer," Slocum decided. The warm, sudsy brew wasn't as likely to hide drugs.

"Two bits," the barkeep said. Slocum paid, not even commenting on the high price. He scanned the room, hunting for the whore he had seen with Beaumont the night before.

"Is Eleanore in? A friend of mine said she's just about the best there is in all San Francisco."

"Eleanore? Don't know any of the girls by that name." The barkeep's face brightened. "Wait, sure I do. Let me go get her. And you're right. She's just about the best there is. I ought to know. I've tried most of 'em."

Slocum watched the bartender hurry toward the cribs. Without appearing to do so, he dropped his hand to his pistol and unhooked the leather thong over the hammer. He wanted to be ready for anything.

The barkeep returned a few minutes later, a whore following closely behind.

"This here's Eleanore. Since she's the best, the price is a dollar in gold, two in scrip."

Slocum stared at her. He hadn't gotten a good look at the woman Beaumont had spoken with, but this one didn't appear to be her. This woman was too thin, too short. When she reached out to take his money, Slocum didn't see the bright red ring on her finger he had noticed before.

"You're not Eleanore," he said.

"Mister, for two dollars I'll be anyone you want. And this Eleanore can't give you want I can. Trust me." She ran her thin fingers up and down his shirtfront. Slocum followed her into the cribs. His shoulders brushed the walls. On the other side of the thin clapboard partitions he heard the grunts and moans of men enjoying themselves.

"It's safe back here," the whore said. She started to unfasten her dress. Slocum stopped her. The woman's eyes grew wide. "Look, mister, we got bouncers. No strange stuff is allowed." She turned shifty when she added in a lower voice, "Leastwise, unless you want to pay for it."

Slocum pulled out two more dollar bills. He folded them lengthwise and held them out for her. Just as she touched them, he pulled back. "I want information. Where can I find the real Eleanore?"

"Mister, I don't know anyone by that name. Not that works here." She sniffed.

"Who do you know named Eleanore?"

"Eleanore Lexington, but she's high-class. She's got her fancy-ass house up on Nob Hill, but don't let that fool you. She sells it just like I do."

"Only she gets more for it?" Slocum asked.

"She might be the one you want, but I doubt it," the woman said, glaring at Slocum.

"Who worked here last night? Emy and Claudia and . . ." He let his voice trail off.

"Only Sheree. She tells everyone she's a hoity-toity from Paris, France. Fact is, she ain't been out of California in her life. Her ma's a gold camp whore, and her father? Who knows."

"She and Beaumont close?"

"Who's Beaumont?" Slocum described his one-time

partner in crime to her. From the way her eyes widened slightly, Slocum knew she had seen him in the Slaughterhouse. "Could be the gent what's been spending time with Sheree."

"Where do I find her?"

"Two dollars ain't much for information."

Slocum silently added another bill. Five dollars was a fortune for a dockside prostitute.

The bills vanished down the front of the woman's bodice. "She's got a place in a boardinghouse along the bay. Mrs. Wright's, I think it's called. Don't go makin' trouble for Sheree, now. I don't much like the bitch, but that's a good house. Mrs. Wright don't cotton to soiled doves staying there. She thinks Sheree's some sort of heiress."

"From France," Slocum finished.

"Yeah, from France," the whore echoed. She turned sullen. "You don't want *any*thing from me? You paid for it. You might as well—"

"Nothing," Slocum said. The stench in the cribs almost overpowered him. He wasn't the most fastidious man in the world, but getting laid in the Slaughterhouse was not to his liking. He started out, only to stop in the narrow corridor leading back to the main saloon.

Standing in the hallway was the bald-headed crimp. He and his friend were dragging some luckless wight from a tiny room. For an instant Slocum didn't think they saw him. Then recognition dawned on the bald man's face. He dropped the shoulders of his shanghai victim and bellowed, "It's him! They didn't keep him on board!"

Slocum drew and fired in a smooth motion. The bald man staggered and fell. Slocum didn't think he had killed him. From the bull-throated roar that rose from him after he hit the floor, he was only enraged, not seriously injured.

Seeing that he wasn't likely to get past the crimps, Slocum spun and raced to the rear of the cribs. A tiny window gave the only exit. He heaved and got it raised, then scrambled through. The pounding of boots inside the saloon told him he didn't have much time—and he sure as hell didn't have enough ammunition to fight off the small army coming after him.

Hitting the dock, he ran for his life. He had enough information to go on. It had cost him dearly, but he didn't mind. He had traded five dollars and might recover almost a thousand from the robbery. But Slocum was worried that Beaumont might have meant someone other than the saloon whore. He might have been calling out for a long-lost lover or who knew who else.

Slocum slowed his pace when he got a few blocks from the saloon. It bothered him that the crimps knew he was still in town. It bothered him even more when he heard a shrill police whistle.

He ducked into an alleyway and reloaded. Four uniformed policemen stormed by, rousting drunks and questioning people in the street. Slocum heard enough of one interrogation to know they were looking for him.

He cursed. The Slaughterhouse Saloon—or the crimps—had set the police on him. The San Francisco police were as corrupt as any law enforcement group in the country. The city paid them nothing. They relied only on what bribes and extortion they could squeeze from those along their beat. And he had never seen them travel in groups smaller than three along the docks.

Ever since the Sydney Ducks had run the city, lawmen had been on the take. And Slocum doubted he had enough money on him to buy them off.

Staying in alleys and taking dark streets, he made his way along the bay until he found Mrs. Wright's Boardinghouse. The whitewashed exterior was neat, clean, and spoke well of its proprietor. A tiny yard filled with blossoming flowers and a tiny patch of green grass showed that this wasn't some flophouse.

Slocum went up the front steps and knocked on the door. When an older, white-haired woman answered, he politely took off his hat and said, "Sorry to bother you this late at night, ma'am."

"I should say so. Why, it is after midnight, sir!" The woman was incensed at his lack of manners. She started to close the door.

"Ma'am, I'm sorry, but this is real important. I have a message for Miss Sheree."

"Miss Dupree?"

"Yes, Miss Dupree," Slocum said smoothly. "I just got a message off a ship that came around the Cape. Her sister is, well, I'd prefer to give her the bad news personally, her being a friend of the family and all."

"Her sister? I did not know Miss Dupree had a sister."

"In France," Slocum said. "In Paris, France."

Mrs. Wright frowned. "You will have to give me the message. I cannot go disturbing her on your say-so."

"I'm truly sorry about this, ma'am," Slocum said. "I feel it's my duty to tell her personally. I'm honor-bound." He saw that he'd hit her soft spot with his plea.

"And I am sorry, sir. Miss Dupree is not here. She left for a society event in Monterey not four hours ago. I have no idea how long she will be gone."

"Monterey?"

"Miss Lexington requested her presence. Miss Dupree was delighted to accept such a gracious invitation."

"I don't know Miss Lexington," he said. "Unless you are referring to Miss *Eleanore* Lexington."

"I am, sir. She is a high-society doyenne, of the very

highest class, mind you. She is the very sort I like to see my boarders have as friends."

"I'm sure," said Slocum. He had found a connection between Sheree Dupree, saloon whore, and Eleanore Lexington, high-society whore. What it meant was beyond him.

"Sir, if you give me the message, I will see that she receives it when she returns. I know it is of a sad nature."

"Her sister died of cholera," Slocum said, making up the story as he told it to Mrs. Wright. "An epidemic swept through Paris. It was sudden. She did not suffer. Her parents sent a more complete account in a packet containing a diary. It is with the shipping agent down at the harbor."

"Her parents? But she said they were deceased."

"Godparents, really," Slocum lied. "Sorry to have disturbed you, ma'am. Please pass the information on to Miss Dupree as quickly as you can. It's not good to let such sorrow go untold."

"Wait! Which shipping agent?"

Slocum donned his hat and almost ran from the porch. Three San Francisco policemen strolled up the well-lit street in front of the boardinghouse.

He found himself trapped in the bright lights of the gas lamps. He didn't dare run off. That would attract the policemen's attention, He settled for a bolder course. He adjusted his Stetson and walked past the three men. Two were swinging nightsticks, and the third walked with his hand on the butt of a pistol thrust into his broad leather belt.

Slocum nodded in their direction and tipped his hat. His hand hid his face, and the shadow from the hat brim did the rest. Heart racing, he walked past, waiting for any hint that they had recognized him.

One policeman mumbled something about a fugitive.

The others doubted their quarry would be in this neighborhood, especially not at Mrs. Wright's door. The woman's fine reputation saved Slocum.

He turned down the first street he came to and quickly vanished from the policemen's sight. Getting back to his hotel unnoticed by crimp or cop—or tong killer—took almost two hours of dodging and hiding in alleys.

San Francisco had become a death trap for John Slocum.

But he wasn't going to leave until he retrieved the money taken from Fah Lu. He had damned well *earned* that money for all he had been through.

5

Slocum flopped onto the narrow brass bed in his hotel room and laced his fingers behind his head. He stared at the ornate lath and plasterwork around the edges of the ceiling. The harder he tried to come to a conclusion about what to do, the worse his confusion became.

The crimps knew he was still in town. They had alerted the police, who traveled everywhere and would reap a healthy reward for finding him. The tong and Fah Lu might even know that he hadn't been successfully shanghaied. Everyone was after him, and any of the three groups would just as soon see him dead.

He should leave San Francisco immediately.

Slocum decided to stay. "Damn it," he said aloud, "that money is *mine*!" With Beaumont and the other two dead, it seemed a waste to let Eleanore Lexington keep it.

Slocum frowned. He didn't actually know that the socialite was the same Eleanore whom Beaumont had mentioned with his last breath. He tried to find another plausible explanation for the dying words and failed. What connection there was between Beaumont, the whore at the saloon, and an obviously well-connected Miss Lexington struck him as dubious. But he knew Beaumont had spoken with Sheree Dupree, who had gone to Monterey at Eleanore Lexington's behest.

He needed more information about the goings-on in Monterey before leaving San Francisco.

"I've got to hide," he said, trying to find clues to survival in his own spoken words. "How? How do I hide when the police and damned near everyone else in the city is looking for me?"

Slocum smiled as the answer came to him. Trying to skulk around on the docks wouldn't work. The crimps knew that territory better than he did. The twilight world of Chinatown along Dupont Gai was similarly closed to him. The police patrolled virtually every street and alley at some time or another in the Barbary Coast and the Battle Row.

The answer came in the "virtually." He knew where he could go and not be seen.

Slocum pulled out the roll of bills he had hidden under the floorboard and counted them again. He still had almost a hundred dollars of carefully saved scrip. He'd put it to good use.

Late the next afternoon he went to a clothing store on Post Street and bought a silvery gray swallowtail coat with velvet tab collars, a ruffled white linen shirt with ebony studs, a grosgrain-ribbon-banded silk top hat, and trousers to match. The price depleted most of his stash, but he didn't worry. He still had more than twenty dollars left. Although this was a modest stake for what he intended, it would have to do.

Dressed in his new finery, he walked unmolested and unnoticed by the police through the city's streets. A few blocks from the Union Club he hailed a cab. The driver looked him over and nodded curtly, approving him as a fare.

"Union Club," Slocum said, settling into the carriage. "On Nob Hill."

"I know where it is. Do you?"

"It's around here somewhere. I've just lost my way," Slocum said, feigning a touch of drunkenness. He wanted to arrive at the club in style while preserving as much of his twenty dollars as possible.

The driver grumbled and decided it wasn't worth driving around for an hour before depositing his besotted charge. The driver let Slocum out less than five minutes later. Slocum tossed him a coin and he drove off.

The perfectly groomed doorman studied Slocum for a moment, then opened the door. The riffraff never entered these sacrosanct premises. It was up to the club's manager to pass judgment on the quality of society passing into the gambling rooms.

"Good evening, sir," the manager said. Slocum felt as if the man had weighed his wallet. "How can I serve you this evening?"

Slocum glanced over the manager's shoulder into the lavishly decorated room holding the gaming tables. Crystal chandeliers gleamed on silver and gold below. Deep-pile Persian carpets kept the patrons' footsteps suitably muffled, to keep them from intruding on each other's concentration as the cards turned and the roulette wheels spun and wooden chips clicked across the green-felt-covered tables.

"I'm looking for a friend of mine," Slocum said, hoping someone would pass by to point at. "We're supposed to do some gambling here this evening."

"You friend's name, sir? I can check to see if he will vouch for you."

"Miss Eleanore Lexington," Slocum said on impulse.

"Oh?" The man's eyebrow arched up just enough to show he didn't believe a word of it.

"Are you badgering Eleanore's friends again, Peterson?" came a gruff voice. "Do you know her well, sir?"

Slocum turned. A florid-faced man stood a pace behind, a lovely young woman on his arm.

"Not well, sir," returned Slocum. "We have a mutual friend. Mr. Beaumont."

"Joshua?" The blonde spoke up at the mention of Beaumont. "I haven't seen him in weeks. Is he to be here tonight?"

"I think not," Slocum said. It startled him that Beaumont was known here.

"Don't worry your head over him, my dear," the ruddy-complected man said. "Peterson, let this gentleman in as my guest. If Harriet knows his friend, and she seems to," he said with ill-concealed disgust, "I certainly know Miss Lexington. Their friends are ours. Come, sir, I'm sure we're both eager to do some serious gambling." The man's arm circled Slocum's shoulders and pulled him past the manager. They swept into the casino.

Its opulence dazzled Slocum. He had been in similar gaming parlors before, but the Union Club surpassed them all. Even the finest Mississippi riverboat casino lacked the elegance displayed here.

The man rushed off before Slocum could thank him. The stunning blonde remained at Slocum's side. She cocked her head to one side and smiled knowingly. "You don't know Eleanore, do you?"

"No," Slocum admitted. "Does it matter?"

"I haven't lost my talent for detecting a lie. And, no, it does not matter. Not to me. Perhaps it does to the colonel." Her blue eyes followed the portly man across the room. He shook hands vigorously with four cigar-smoking men standing at the long teak and gold bar.

"The colonel?"

The woman laughed. "He isn't an Army officer. He just likes the sound of the title. With his money, he can call himself anything he wants." She looked at Slocum again. "Do you know Joshua? Really?"

"I do," Slocum said. "We had . . . business dealings."

"So you're looking to blow his head off?" Seeing Slocum's startled expression, the blonde laughed and took his arm. "That's only a joke, sir. I know how Joshua does business. He never does anything legally if he can do it illegally. Cheating business partners is second nature to him."

"It was that," Slocum agreed. He didn't feel as bad about Beaumont's death as he once had. "How good a gambler was he?"

"Joshua? The man didn't know odds from ends. He bet on ridiculous things—and lost consistently. I saw him lose more than fourteen thousand dollars in one night to the colonel. And *he's* a terrible cardplayer."

Slocum didn't see a wedding ring on the blonde's finger. She noticed his interest. In a soft voice she said, "He's as bad in bed as he is at the gaming table, but he is a generous man."

"Where is Miss Lexington?" Slocum asked, trying not to show too much interest.

The blonde laughed. The sound was musical. Slocum decided the colonel might be a poor gambler but he knew quality in women when he saw it.

"Where is everyone now? They're all getting ready to go to the Del Monte Hotel opening."

"Oh? In Monterey?"

"Where else? How many hotels are opened by Charles Crocker after costing well over one million dollars to construct?"

"Railroad money?" asked Slocum, interested. A million dollars was a fabulous amount to spend on a hotel. Even a man with the railroad magnate's wealth would be hard-pressed to build such an expensive structure.

"You haven't heard of the Pacific Improvement Company?" she asked, startled at his ignorance. "Mr. Crocker and Leland Stanford got the idea of a consortium. They entered into it with Mark Hopkins and Collis Huntington two years ago."

Slocum recognized the names of California's richest citizens. They had made millions in railroading, banking, and outright swindling. A million dollars for the Del Monte Hotel would be insignificant to such a group of men.

"Eleanore is already in Monterey with fifty of her finest." The blonde's lip curled slightly, showing what she thought of Miss Lexington's "finest."

"The grand opening must be exclusive," Slocum said. "How do you get invited to it?"

"Be someone important. Know someone important," she said idly. "There. That's the kind of man they should ban from the club. He's disgusting!"

A seedy-looking man with a beer belly entered the Union Club and looked around. His hair had been slicked back with heavy grease. His cloth coat stood poor comparison with the rich fabric so apparent in the rest of the room. The man's boots were unpolished, and his vest lacked two buttons, letting his soiled shirt poke through.

"He got past Peterson," Slocum said.

"He's the assistant police commissioner. A pig of a man. He probably steals more than anyone else in the room." The blonde tittered and delicately dabbed at her lips with a lace handkerchief. "That'd make him about the richest man in California. But he *is* a pig."

Slocum watched the police official begin the rounds. He lost heavily at a roulette wheel, then moved to a game of seven-card stud. In exchange for covering his losses, the assistant police commissioner allowed the club to operate unrestricted.

"Do you gamble, sir?"

"Of course," Slocum said, thinking how he had entered the club. "I even place a bet now and then."

The blonde laughed in delight at his small witticism. She guided him toward the table where the policeman was playing. Slocum tried to steer her to another game.

"No, don't worry. I can see you don't have much money." She bent over and whispered for a few seconds in the dealer's ear. The man nodded, then gestured to another man behind the bar. He brought a stack of black chips and handed them to Slocum.

"Thousand-dollar chips," the blonde said. "Enjoy yourself. I charged it against the colonel's account. Oh, don't worry," she said when she saw Slocum start to protest. "He'll never notice. His bill here is always sooo high."

She stared at him boldly. "I'd like to get to know you better—if you have the nerve."

"Let me see how the cards turn. Lady Luck hasn't been with me lately."

"She is . . . now."

Slocum sat two chairs to the right of the assistant police commissioner. The man cast him a sidelong glance that made Slocum edgy. A flicker of recognition traveled behind the policeman's light gray eyes. He said nothing as the dealer laid down another round of cards. Slocum's nervousness faded when he saw the cards and got into the play.

He was aware of the blonde's hand on his shoulder as he played and won, but nothing else disturbed him.

"You wanting to make that large a bet, sir?" asked the dealer. "It is five thousand over our table limit."

Slocum didn't bother looking at his cards. He knew he

had a straight and was likely to beat anyone else at the table. Nodding, he said, "I'd like to let it ride, if I can. If not . . ." He shrugged, showing it didn't matter to him.

From the bar came a single word: yes.

Play continued, and Slocum won almost nine thousand dollars. He pulled the chips in and counted out ten of them.

"Here's the colonel's money back," Slocum said, "with interest." He added an eleventh chip.

The blonde smiled at him. "This is the easiest money he's made in months and months." She passed the chips to the manager, who took them without comment.

"I'd like to buy you a drink," Slocum said, pushing back from the table. Seven of the black chips and a handful of blues remained in front of him. He pushed the blues—five hundred dollars—toward the dealer as a tip. The man's eyes widened, and he smiled. The chips vanished into an inner pocket faster than a striking rattler hits its target.

"A moment," called the corpulent assistant police commissioner. "Why'd you give the dealer any money? You weren't cheating, now were you?"

"Really, sir," the blonde cut in. "How dare you suggest such a thing? My friend was merely being polite and thanking Lady Luck for his winning streak."

"Why'd you give the dealer money?" the policeman demanded. "The two of you been cheatin' the rest of us?"

"What were your losses?" asked Slocum. "I'll be glad to reimburse you, if you think there was any problem." Slocum knew the police official didn't have any losses, that the Union Club swallowed them to keep on the good side of the San Francisco police.

"I'm Jakey Leonard, assistant police commissioner," the fat man declared. He bumped up against Slocum with his belly. Slocum felt a quiver of revulsion at the man's touch.

He wished he had worn his Colt Navy, although it would have been a detriment to getting into the club. All he had was a double-shot .44 derringer tucked into a vest pocket.

"He's the colonel's guest," the blonde said, her ire rising. Slocum liked the way fire came into her normally cool blue eyes. "He's also friends with Joshua Beaumont. *They* are members in good standing in this club."

The policeman ignored her. "You friends with that no-account Beaumont? Haven't seen him around since he ran up more of his gambling debts. How do you know him?"

Slocum realized he knew little about Joshua Beaumont's lifestyle. He had thought Beaumont was simply another money-hungry man looking to add quick gold to his pocket by robbing the opium den. Slocum now saw that Beaumont had financed his high living by such mad ventures. From all the colonel's companion had hinted about Beaumont, he had intended to leave Slocum and the other two high and dry—and in deep trouble with Fah Lu and the tong.

"Excuse me, sir," Slocum said, offering his arm to the lady. "Winning has made me thirsty."

"You cheated." The words echoed across the suddenly silent room. All eyes turned to Assistant Police Commissioner Leonard. "You and that jackanapes dealer cheated the rest of us."

"I did not—*we* did not," Slocum said coldly. "Since there is some dispute on the point, I insist on turning all my winnings back to the house."

"Don't," the blonde protested. "He can't prove anything, because you weren't cheating."

Leonard shoved her out of the way. The manager, Peterson, and two well-dressed, burly men who were obviously bouncers silently appeared behind the policeman.

"What is the problem, Commissioner?" asked Peterson.

"Caught this one cheating. I think he ought to be run in while we investigate the matter."

"Did I hear you say he was in collusion with one of my dealers?" Peterson's keen eyes shifted to the dealer. The man sat, face white and his eyes round. He shook his head.

"Maybe not. Maybe he did it all on his own."

"Is this the way you run your club, sir?" the blonde demanded of the manager. "Do you allow ruffians such as . . . *him* to push around ladies of breeding?"

"You a lady of breeding?" scoffed Leonard. "You're nothing but one of Eleanore Lexington's cheap whores, and everybody in the damned room knows it."

Slocum hoped the colonel would come to the woman's defense. The argument would shift from him, and he could ease out of the Union Club and hightail it out of San Francisco. He cursed under his breath when he saw that the colonel had gone into the back rooms with three cronies. Slocum remained firmly in the center of the raging storm.

"You are both fat and insulting," Slocum said in a voice too low for anyone but Leonard to hear.

"Outside, you son of a bitch!" Leonard grabbed Slocum's collar and jerked him hard. Cloth tore. No one sprang to his defense as the bloated police official gave Slocum the bum's rush out of the club.

Slocum let the policeman unceremoniously escort him out a side door. More than maintaining his dignity, he wanted to be away from the prying eyes of the Union Club members. When the door slammed behind them and the cold San Francisco night air struck him in the face like a blow, Slocum swung around and caught Leonard's thick wrist.

Twisting hard, he broke the police commissioner's grip and forced him to his knees.

"You need to be taught manners," Slocum said. He

wanted nothing more than to leave. He had the information he had come to the club for. "I'm going to let you go, if you apologize."

"Bastard!" roared the police official. "You're the one them crimps are looking for. Fah Lu and his tong friends want your head on a platter. The whole damned town's after you. You got a five-thousand-dollar reward riding on you, damn it!"

Slocum cursed. The man had recognized him in the club. The argument over cheating at cards had been a ruse to get him outside. Leonard didn't want to split the reward offered by Fah Lu with Peterson or anyone in the Union Club, as if they would have wanted it.

Grunting like a hog in a wallow, Jakey Leonard drove forward from his knees. His log-thick arms circled Slocum's knees and forced him to the ground. The assistant police commissioner rose up like an avenging angel. Something silver flashed in his hand.

Slocum didn't stop to wonder what it was. He drew his derringer and fired. The heavy .44 slug wasn't accurate. At point-blank range it didn't have to be. The lead slug caught Leonard square in the chest and lifted him up and back.

He fell to the ground, lifeless.

Slocum cursed his continued bad luck. Beaumont had tricked him and stolen the money they had taken from the opium parlor, he had been shanghaied, and now he had signed his own death warrant in San Francisco by killing a police official. The tong *and* the police would be after his blood now.

The only spot of luck he had had was in the steady wind blowing across the knoll where the Union Club stood. The whistle of the wind from the Pacific had drowned out much of the sharp report from the derringer.

Slocum didn't see anyone watching. He dropped down

beside the police official and rummaged through his pockets. He found a wallet stuffed with crumpled bills. He took them, deciding Leonard owed him something for leaving his winnings back on the table in the casino. He might as well be hung for a thief and a murderer instead of just a murderer.

A gilt-edged envelope caught his eye. Slocum held it up to the light coming from the front of the Union Club. A florid hand had written the assistant police commissioner's name across the front. Intrigued, Slocum opened the envelope and studied the engraved invitation.

He smiled as he pocketed the invitation to the opening of the Del Monte Hotel. Jakey Leonard couldn't attend, but John Slocum would go in his stead.

6

John Slocum didn't bother returning to his hotel room to stay. Sneaking in through an upstairs window, he retrieved his Colt Navy and trail clothes. To sleep here invited being murdered in the middle of night. He decided that the police might have tracked him down to that lair. If they hadn't, the On Leong tong killers would have. He wished he had settled in a hotel farther away from Portsmouth Square and Fah Lu's opium den. When he had reached San Francisco he didn't have any notion of getting involved in such a robbery.

He took his pitiful belongings and wandered along the streets paralleling Portsmouth Square until he found a small boardinghouse set on a cul-de-sac. Slocum took the chance that one more night spent here wouldn't be too dangerous. Dressed as he was in the silver-gray swallowtail and top hat, he had no trouble convincing the woman running the establishment that he was a slightly drunk businessman who refused to go home in his besotted condition.

Half the night Slocum spent trying to decide what to do next. He thought hard as he cleaned his six-shooter and derringer. If he had a lick of sense he'd find a livery, buy a horse, and ride on out of San Francisco.

He was in too deep for that. The police might not chase him far for the death of their assistant police commissioner, but the tong would follow him to hell and beyond to recover their money now that they knew he was alive. Slocum considered that for a spell. Nothing would stop them. He doubted that even if he found the money Beaumont had hidden and returned it to Fah Lu it would be enough. He shrugged it off.

He had no plans to return money gotten by selling opium to hopheads.

Getting out from under the police was another matter. They would be watching the harbors and train stations.

Slocum sprawled back on the bed and thought on this. Would they? Did they even know *he* had killed Jakey Leonard? Leonard had spotted him in the Union Club because the crimps had put out the reward for him. The police had no reason to connect him with the police official's death, except through the description of those inside the club. No matter what, they'd want to talk to him. And he knew how they "talked" to their prisoners.

A daring plan came to him as he fingered Leonard's invitation to the Del Monte Hotel gala. He fell asleep with a smile on his lips.

The next morning he spent a goodly portion of the money he had taken from the slain police commissioner on a morning coat and appropriate accoutrements. He summoned a passing carriage for hire and told the driver, "The Central Pacific station. The charter train for Monterey."

"You, sir?" The driver turned and studied Slocum too closely for comfort. He shrugged and applied the reins to the horse. They clattered off in the direction of the train station to the south of town.

When Slocum left the carriage he saw why the driver had sounded so skeptical. A crowd of well-dressed ladies stood on the platform. Slocum guessed this train was conveying the painted women Eleanore Lexington had hired for the gala. Slocum decided his luck wasn't that bad, after all. Who would give him a second glance in this company?

"May I help you, sir?" asked the train conductor. Slocum saw that the man's uniform had been repaired recently. The patches showing which railroad he worked for had been removed and replaced with Central Pacific insignia.

"I've been invited to the Del Monte Hotel," he said, presenting his gilt-edged invitation with a flourish. He hoped the conductor wouldn't examine the name on the envelope too closely. A man as powerful as Jakey Leonard would be well known to most people in San Francisco.

"Very good, sir. We hadn't expected any but the ladies and a few others this early in the day, but we can accommodate you. Where is your luggage?"

"I'm traveling light," Slocum said, explaining away his dearth of baggage. "What happened to your uniform? It appears you've changed companies."

The expression on the conductor's face told Slocum that the man was not happy with the change. "Last year the Monterey and Salinas Valley Railroad had a series of fires. Mr. Jacks, the owner, was forced to sell as a result."

"To the Central Pacific?"

"Yes, sir. Mr. Crocker and Mr. Stanford were kind enough to go to the Southern Pacific Railroad's board of directors and authorize the money for the purchase." The conductor's tone told Slocum that the men had caused David Jacks's problems to get him to sell the narrow-gauge line.

Everyone knew that the Central Pacific and the Southern Pacific were Crocker's to do with as he saw fit.

"How is it you don't know this, sir?" asked the conductor. Slocum wanted to keep him from looking more closely at the invitation.

"I've been away on business," he lied. "Although it was

quite profitable, it kept me away from San Francisco and all that has been happening here."

"Yes, sir." The conductor had already lost interest in him. A bevy of Miss Lexington's ladies had come onto the platform and pulled the man's eyes to more attractive items. "The porter will show you to a first-class car."

Slocum nodded and watched as the conductor hurried to help the women. For the man who had had his old railroad burned out from under him, this trip might be compensation enough.

A Negro porter showed Slocum to a compartment lavish enough for a visiting head of state. Slocum settled into the plush wine-red-velvet cushions and decided he could get to like this life. He pulled down the shades until only a thin sliver of light entered. He didn't bother turning up the gaslight.

All he wanted was for the train to pull out of San Francisco and head for Monterey. And he wanted it even more when he saw a squad of policemen burst onto the platform. They scattered the women in all directions as they roughly pushed their way through the crowd. The conductor argued with them—and lost.

Slocum reached under his morning coat and touched the Colt Navy he had thrust into his waistband. It might be used sooner than he had thought.

The police studied every man on the platform, then entered the train at the rear. Slocum guessed they were starting to search the train at the last car and moving forward. His compartment was three or four cars behind the engine. He considered getting into the cramped passageway and finding a way off before the police got to him.

Those hopes were dashed when he heard nightsticks cracking against doors and the rough commands from the policemen to open up. Slocum had only a few seconds before they reached his compartment.

He stood to open the sliding door. A second of shock at seeing a Colt thrust into their faces might win him the time he needed to make a run for it.

Slocum doubted it. Blood would flow—soon.

A sharp rap came at his door. He slid it open and started to pull his six-shooter on the policemen. A commotion behind the two officers caused them to look back. A short, impeccably dressed woman shoved them aside and blocked their view of Slocum. She planted her feet squarely on the floor and threw her arms around his neck.

Slocum found himself smothered by her kisses. "It's so good seeing you again! I know it was only last night, but I've been so lonely. I miss you when you leave me like that. What are these nasty men doing here? Don't they know it's not nice to disturb a director of the Southern Pacific Railroad?"

"Sorry, ma'am, sir," the policeman nearest Slocum said. He tipped his bucket-like hat and moved on, looking frightened at the prospect of disturbing such a powerful man and his mistress.

The woman shoved Slocum back into the compartment. In a loud voice she said, "The trip to Monterey is going to be *so* much fun with you." As she continued shoving him into the plush seats, she hooked the door with the toe of her shoe and closed it smartly.

Slocum simply stared. He had been ready for gunplay and death, not to be buried alive with passionate kisses.

"You owe me for this one," the woman said. She pulled the long veil over her face and tossed her head twice and got free of her wide-brimmed hat. Cascades of long, lustrous blonde hair fell out. The woman who had been with the colonel at the Union Club had inexplicably come to his rescue.

"Thanks," Slocum said.

"We were never properly introduced last night," she said almost primly. "I am Harriet Griffith."

"I'm—"

She didn't give him the chance to finish. "You're most certainly not that pig of an assistant police commissioner." She reached into his inner coat pocket and fished out his invitation and stared at the envelope with Leonard's name on it. "You really should have substituted another envelope with your name. Or better yet . . ." Harriet tore up the envelope, turned up the compartment's gas lamp, and thrust the pieces into the low flame until only soot remained.

"Why did you save me from the police?"

"Why did you kill Leonard?" she shot back. Harriet settled on the plush seat next to him.

Slocum inhaled and smelled the sweet, intoxicating perfume the woman used. It turned him giddy in the small compartment. "He didn't give me much choice."

"Peterson alibied for you," Harriet said. "The police got a description of you from a driver who delivered you to the club. You only rode a few blocks?" Harriet laughed. Again came a sound more pleasant than silver bells in a spring breeze.

"Why did the club manager bother?"

"The colonel told him to. Because I asked the colonel to," she answered before he even put the question to her. "I took quite a fancy to you, Mr. Slocum."

He heaved a deep sigh. Even his name was on the arrest warrant. Thoughts of giving up on recovering the money stolen from Fah Lu flashed through his head.

"Most of the men at the Union Club are so dreary. Fat,

boring, always talking business and how hard they work. You are different. You are . . . dangerous."

"You like that?" he asked, still considering getting off the train after it had gone a few miles out of San Francisco.

"I hate tedious people," Harriet said. She took a tortoiseshell comb from her bag and used it on her long, flowing hair. "You did kill Leonard, didn't you?"

"Yes." Slocum saw no reason to deny it. "He decided he would rather take me in dead than alive. It was self-defense."

"I thought so. He had a reputation for being a vicious brute. I never liked him, especially when he tried to . . . Never mind." Harriet turned and faced the rear of the train and continued combing her lustrous blonde hair.

"Is the colonel with you?"

"He has to stay in San Francisco on business." Harriet paused and stared at him, her bright blue eyes shining. "You have guessed that I work for Eleanore, haven't you?"

Slocum's heart almost blasted from his chest. He had wondered how to get in touch with Eleanore Lexington once he arrived at the Del Monte Hotel. Through Harriet he could learn what Beaumont had done with the money.

"In what capacity? You're not just a . . ." He didn't know how to politely phrase what he wanted to say.

"Just another painted lady?" Harriet laughed. "Not that. None of Eleanore's employees are that. We're more discreet. Eleanore Lexington has immense power in San Francisco—through others like me." Harriet dropped her elaborate lace shawl and took off her long black traveling gloves. "We find men of power and wealth, such as the colonel, and accompany them. We hear things. We make contacts that prove important to Eleanore."

"She has a spy in every corner of San Francisco society."

"Perhaps not in *society*," Harriet said. "Certainly not polite society. But we serve as confidantes of those who do enter that arena. The colonel tells me the most outrageous things—things he would never mention to his wife."

"I see." Slocum looked under the window blind and saw the policemen forming their ranks again. They had come up empty-handed. For that he could only thank Harriet. Without her timely intervention, he would have been rotting in a cell, wondering whether the tong or the crimps would kill him first.

"It has its benefits," Harriet said. She licked her ruby lips. Then she began unfastening the high-buttoned collar to her expensive dress. "I thought the trip to Monterey would be boring. I know it won't be now."

The train lurched and began to build up speed. A loud whistle sounded as the engine pulled its load out of the station. Slocum hardly noticed. His eyes were on Harriet Griffith. She tossed aside her gloves and skinned out of her dress. The corset she wore rose and cupped soft white breasts. Poking over the rim of the corset's whalebone ridge were two hard, pink nipples.

"Go on," Harriet said in her soft, sexy voice. "You want to suck on them, don't you? Go on. I want it too."

She thrust her chest forward. Slocum forgot about leaving the train and running for his life. He could leave at Monterey as easily as he could anywhere along the train's route.

And the trip was proving to be more entertaining than he had believed possible.

He dropped to his knees and licked lightly over her left nipple. She purred like a contented cat with a bowl of cream. He repeated the oral laving on her right. His tongue burrowed down into the frilled corset and teased the nipple out fully so that his lips brushed across it. Slocum felt the woman's pulse pounding hard through the tiny button of aroused flesh.

"Don't stop there," Harriet urged. "Undo the laces. With your teeth!"

Slocum started working down the front of her securely laced corset, using tongue and teeth to pull the ties free. He worked as quickly as he could, but it wasn't fast enough for Harriet.

She completed the job for him and shrugged out of the corset. She sprawled back wantonly on the deep red velvet seat. She lifted her hips and worked off the rest of her skirt and undergarments until she was naked in front of him.

"Your turn," she said. Her eyes had turned a deeper blue. Her chest heaved and set her breasts to quivering in tempo with the movement caused by the rocking train. "Hurry. Please hurry!"

Slocum couldn't get out of his fancy duds fast enough for her. She pulled and tugged and helped him. When his trousers opened, Harriet's mouth encircled the already rigid length she found there. Slocum gasped and almost fell when she began applying a gentle suction to the tip of his manhood. His legs turned weak. He had to sink down and sit on the edge of the seat across from the woman.

"You like this, don't you?" she asked needlessly. His response to her pursued lips was obvious.

As the train lurched, Slocum changed seats. His arms circled the willing woman and pulled her close. Her soft breasts with their hard nipples crushed against his bare chest. Their mouths locked firmly in a deep, passionate kiss. Slocum's nostrils flared as he inhaled Harriet's subtle perfume mixed with the musky odors of her desire.

He gasped as she gripped his lust-hardened length and tugged him toward her.

"In," she begged. "I need you inside me. And don't try

moving. Just sit still and let the train's movement do it all."

"That doesn't seem too interesting," Slocum said.

"You haven't done it before, have you?" Harriet spun around and faced him, her thighs parting widely. She knelt on either side of his legs, straddling him. She lowered herself slowly.

They both gasped when his engorged tip touched the gates of her inner paradise. For a moment, Harriet hung suspended, savoring the sensations wracking her. Then she sank down, taking his full length easily.

Slocum thought he was going to lose control. He was surrounded by hot, moist, wanton female flesh. And he saw instantly what she meant by letting the motion of the train do the work.

Simply sitting on the velvet turned into excitement almost too much for him. As the train rocked around bends and simply rattled along on its wheels, a vibration passed through the floor, his legs, the seat, and into their joined crotches.

When Harriet began twisting slowly from side to side Slocum knew he couldn't hang on much longer. The blonde saw this and started moving up and down on his cock. Her lips crushed his. They clutched each other fiercely.

Slocum felt the hot tide rising in his loins. When it erupted and was swallowed within Harriet's passionate depths, the woman cried out. She clung to him with a intensity that was not to be denied.

Grinding crotch to crotch, they soared on the winds of mutually shared desire. Even after Harriet relaxed and slumped forward against him, Slocum felt the effect of the rattling train wheels communicated up through their bodies. Never had he been stirred from the inside out before.

"I'm definitely going to enjoy the trip to Monterey," Harriet said as she nibbled at his ear. "How about you?"

Slocum answered her sooner than he would have thought possible.

7

The three-hour trip on the train from San Francisco proved all too short for John Slocum. Still, he was exhausted by Harriet's insatiable sexual demands by the time the train pulled to a halt in the Monterey station.

Harriet primly fixed her dress and smoothed away wrinkles. She donned her long black traveling gloves and critically studied herself in the window's reflection. She liked what she saw. So did Slocum.

"It's time to get to work," she said, heaving a deep sigh.

"Do you have to?" asked Slocum. "You're beautiful. You can do whatever you want."

"Eleanore has been good to me. When I arrived in San Francisco, I was starving to death. My family had died just after we rounded Cape Horn. Dysentery. Bad food. I don't know. I survived and ended up fifteen years old and on my own." Her sudden bitterness told Slocum that she was reliving old and unpleasant memories.

He reached out and touched her cheek.

She pulled back. "Don't," she said. "I've enjoyed this. Now I have to go keep the customers satisfied for the week."

"Week?"

"The Del Monte Hotel's grand opening is just that—grand. Mr. Crocker intends to have an entire week of celebration." She shuddered. "He plans to keep everyone *very* happy to show how good a businessman he is."

"And you're to do that?"

"Of course. That's why Eleanore pays me so well." Harriet Griffith stood and settled her wide-brimmed hat on her head, tucking up blonde locks beneath it. She dropped her long veil and became anonymous. She lifted the veil for a moment and lightly kissed him. "Don't run off. No one will look for you here. Stay. Please."

With that she dashed from the compartment. For a fleeting instant Slocum wondered if any of the last three hours had even happened. The lingering scent of her perfume convinced him that it had. He adjusted his own clothing and wiped off a smear of lip rouge that had turned his cheek to a blush, and he made certain his Colt Navy was close at hand. Satisfied, he left the train.

The women who had taken the train were already clustered on the Monterey station platform. Tallyhos from the hotel awaited them. The women sat four to a carriage. The crack of whips and the whinnying of horses told Slocum how well organized this venture was. In minutes the last of Eleanore Lexington's ladies had been spirited away.

The stationmaster came out and looked him over. Seeing the finery the grizzled old railroad man asked, "You one of the guests over at Mr. Crocker's fancy place?"

"Reckon so," Slocum said. "I need to find some transportation to the hotel."

"That's supposed to be taken care of." The stationmaster spat, scratched his head, and looked at a sheaf of papers he was clutching. He shook his head. "You ain't supposed to be in till tomorrow. The main opening's the first Saturday in June. That's what my orders say. A special train's coming down then with all the dignitaries."

"I came early," Slocum said.

"You a guest? You're not with the . . . ladies?"

"I don't work at the hotel," Slocum said.

"Damnation. They're always making life hard for me. I'll scare you up a carriage and driver. You just cool your heels a spell and let me tend to it."

Slocum saw a red-haired urchin come running from the stationmaster's office a few seconds after the man vanished inside. The boy was running as if his shirttail had caught fire.

The stationmaster came back outside and rejoined Slocum. "He'll fetch someone. Offer you a drink?" The railroad man pulled out a hip flash and popped out the cork with a loud *thwap!*

"Why not? The trip was mighty tiring," Slocum said.

"If'n you'd come tomorrow, they'd've stuffed you with food and given you enough liquor to float a steam engine." The stationmaster gestured toward a pair of chairs. Slocum took one and the man settled in the other. "I reckon you enjoyed the trip down here a mite more'n any of them will."

Slocum allowed as to how he had. The liquor burned his gullet and pooled warmly in his stomach. "You know any of the ladies?" Slocum asked. He wanted to find Sheree Dupree and find what Joshua Beaumont had done with the money. Then he could get the hell away.

In spite of his intentions, he found himself thinking about Harriet Griffith. He'd miss the blonde, even though he had known her only a short while. She definitely had a way about her that pleased him mightily.

The stationmaster laughed. "Them folks are out of my league." The old railroad man cocked his head to one side and squinted at Slocum. "You don't strike me as being like them either. You just tryin' to get in on some free food and liquor over at the hotel?"

"Something like that," Slocum said. He had no reason

to lie. The stationmaster wasn't likely to tell anyone what was said on the platform in the heat of a fine summer day.

"Don't go gettin' tangled up with the likes of Mr. Crocker. He's one mean son of a bitch. That's how he got as rich as he has."

"I heard about David Jacks's misfortune."

"Some misfortune. They burned him out. They hired away his best men, then cut rates so he couldn't compete on that narrow gauge. The turncoat farmers all went over to Mr. Crocker's line." The stationmaster spat again. "Can't rightly blame them, though. They get lower rates, why not jump ship and go with a competitor? Laugh is on them, nowadays. Crocker's pushed their shipping costs higher'n the sky."

Slocum saw a tallyho returning from the Del Monte Hotel. Sitting beside the driver was the redheaded boy who had rushed out.

"That was a quick trip."

"Not more'n a quarter mile over. That kid knows all the shortcuts in these parts. He's been showin' a writer fellow around."

"A writer?"

"Some British fellow. Scots, actually. Name of Stevenson. He made quite a hit over in Monterey. Can't see how being able to scribble down a few words makes you that much more of a person. He cadged free meals and lodging the whole time he was here."

"He's gone?"

"He and his lady friend from Oakland left for Tahiti or some such place a week back. A pity. He was a keen observer on politics in these parts. He'd've got a laugh or two out of the Del Monte's opening."

Slocum bade the railroad man farewell and climbed in.

The driver looked startled when he saw how little gear Slocum had with him.

"I always travel light," Slocum explained. The driver shrugged. It wasn't any business of his how his passengers traveled as long as he got them to the gala in time.

The Del Monte Hotel appeared suddenly through the stand of trees near the coastline. Slocum mistook it for a bank of fog at first. He didn't believe anything could be so lovely and so large. The pearl-gray of the walls matched his morning coat exactly. Turrets rose here and there on the two-story structure, and great wings extended from the main building.

"It's Swiss-Gothic," the driver said, seeing his interest. "Mr. Crocker put it smack dab in the middle of a one-hundred-and-twenty-six-acre forest."

Slocum looked around. Everywhere he looked he saw pine and oak forest, but the grounds were what startled him the most. Flower beds blazed with color. The seven-foot-high topiary hedge made Slocum uneasy. The animal shapes shifted slightly in the sea breeze off the Pacific.

"What's that ahead?" he asked.

"The glass-roofed building? That's the bathing pavilion. The finest baths south of San Francisco," the driver said proudly. "There are four saltwater bathing pools, each at a different temperature."

"What does it cost to stay at a place like this? After the grand opening," Slocum said quickly.

"Three dollars a day and up," the driver said. Such a princely sum required lavish facilities.

Slocum jumped down from the carriage and walked up the flagstone steps to the front doors, which were highly polished wood with inset stained glass. He entered the lobby of the hotel and found himself in a new world, a better world. Slocum had been in fine hotels before. He had thought the Union Club was superb. But the Del Monte Hotel made the Union Club and the others on Nob Hill seem tawdry in comparison.

"This way, sir," said a uniformed attendant. Slocum followed to the registration desk. He hesitated to flash the assistant police commissioner's invitation. Too many here might know the officials in San Francisco. Jakey Leonard had been such a son of a bitch, few would forget having met him—or run afoul of him.

"Here," Slocum said, smoothly presenting the invitation and hoping they wouldn't ask for the burned envelope. "I'm sorry about coming a day early. I got the dates wrong."

"That's not a problem to worry about, sir. May I have your name? We have assigned suites already." The clerk waited as Slocum began to sweat. What did he say? What if the clerk knew the assistant police commissioner by sight?

"Oh, there you are, my dear. I wondered what kept you," came a dulcet voice he remembered well. Harriet hurried over from across the large lobby. She took his arm and snuggled close. "Have you completed this tiresome check-in yet?"

"I need the gentleman's name, ma'am," the clerk said. Slocum knew from the clerk's tone that he didn't know Harriet's name but knew why she was here.

"Leonard," Slocum said without hesitation. He felt Harriet tense at his side.

"Yes, sir, we have you in room 2118, south wing, second floor. A fine room, sir, overlooking the bay and the ocean. I am sure you will find it to your liking."

"Let's go look at it," cooed Harriet. She looked around, then shook her head. "Where's your luggage? Don't tell me they haven't found it yet." She made a face and turned to the clerk. "Be sure his luggage is sent directly to the room when it arrives. Can you imagine? They *lost* it!"

"Sir!" the clerk cried, aggrieved at such inefficiency. "If there is anything you require, please tell a bellman. The Del Monte Hotel will provide it to you at no expense."

"Fine, thank you. I will be needing another change of clothing." At this he heard Harriet try to hold back a chuckle. Slocum saw no reason not to take full advantage of his position of being a traveler stranded without luggage.

Slocum turned from the clerk and saw a woman who could only be Sheree Dupree across the lobby. He started toward her, but Harriet held him back. Hesitation flared. He didn't want to abandon the lovely blonde, yet he had to speak with Sheree if he ever wanted the money from the opium den robbery.

"Let's explore a bit before going to the room," he suggested. He guided Harriet in the direction taken by Sheree. Voices echoed through the immense structure. They passed a large dining room.

"It's large enough for seven hundred and fifty people," Harriet said. "You'd think they were feeding an army instead of a distinguished few."

"If this opening is as large as it seems, that might not be big enough."

"You're very foolhardy," she said, changing the subject. "You should have picked a name at random rather than using Leonard's. Killing an assistant police commissioner is a serious offense. Word will get out, even at a gala like this. The police commissioner himself has been invited."

Slocum shrugged it off. He took chances all the time. This seemed less risky than picking a name and bluffing his way into the hotel.

He craned his neck to see around a corner into a sitting

room. Wing-top Morris chairs filled the space in front of a huge fireplace. Small tables were placed around the room for drinks. At first he didn't see Sheree. Then he heard a woman's laughter and saw the flash of her hair over the top of a chair turned toward a window.

"Don't," Harriet said. "Don't interrupt. He's one mean bastard."

Slocum saw the man Sheree was sitting with and saw what Harriet meant. A large scar ran diagonally across the man's face from his upper left temple down to his right jaw. How he had sustained such a wound and not lost an eye was a mystery Slocum didn't want to explore.

"Who is he?"

"Max Thorvald. He's a shipping magnate. He owns dozens of China clippers. He might even be a partner in the Pacific Improvement Company, though I doubt it. Charles Crocker and Leland Stanford use the PIC as a holding company for their personal fortunes."

Slocum watched from across the room as Sheree talked intimately with Thorvald and laughed at his jokes. He was itching to recover Fah Lu's stolen money and be on his way. He saw that any interruption now would cause more ruckus than it was worth. He would have to find Sheree later.

"What's your interest in her?" Harriet asked somewhat sourly. "What's she got that I don't?"

"Nothing," Slocum lied. Physically Sheree didn't hold a candle to Harriet Griffith. They were from different worlds. But the other woman might know where Beaumont had hidden the money. That made a big difference. With the money Slocum knew he could actually afford a few nights in such a fine place as the Del Monte Hotel.

"Let's go to the billiards room, or perhaps you prefer bowling. I can watch. You must be good at things other than the ones you've demonstrated," Harriet said coyly.

"Billiards? Bowling?" Slocum was distracted by Sheree and Thorvald and paid the lovely woman scant attention.

"There are separate buildings housing an alley and tables. Come, I'll show you. Eleanore is most thorough. She told us all about the hotel before we left San Francisco so we wouldn't seem like complete dolts."

Slocum let the blonde lead him away. He cursed his bad luck in not being able to get to Sheree Dupree. That luck had to change later—if being with Harriet Griffith could ever be called bad luck.

8

John Slocum went out onto the balcony of his second-floor room and stared across the Pacific Ocean. Almost at his feet a small bay housed several fishing boats. Farther out, he saw the three soaring masts of a Cape ship. Whitecaps had formed in the ocean because of the wind blowing in more strongly now that it was nearing sunset. He leaned on the iron rail and looked down into the Del Monte Hotel's grounds.

They had been perfectly styled. The grass lawn appeared smooth enough to shoot billiards on. The hedges with the animal shapes cut into them still bothered him. The gentle breeze moved the animal shapes; somehow the hedges spooked him.

He tried to isolate the real cause of his uneasiness. It might be Max Thorvald's continued attention to Sheree. The shipping magnate had not left her side all afternoon. Slocum had considered sending the man one beer after another. Only Harriet's sarcastic remarks had drawn him away from the sitting room.

He had to retrieve the stolen money. The pressure of time squeezed him like white-hot pincers. Every minute he stayed at the Del Monte Hotel increased the chance someone who knew Jakey Leonard would expose his small charade.

Tomorrow might be the worst, Slocum knew. The six-car train was due in from San Francisco at ten in the morning. Aboard would be Charles Crocker, Collis Huntington, and Leland Stanford. Mark Hopkins would follow in a few days, so that all the partners in the Pacific Improvement Company would be present during the week. With them came the cream of San Francisco society—and the dregs.

Men like Max Thorvald hired crimps. Slocum had seen many of the servants. They were mostly Chinese. How many had ties with Fah Lu or the On Leong tong? He didn't want to think about that. And what would Crocker and the others do to him if they found he had killed San Francisco's assistant police commissioner? Everywhere he looked he saw the dark clouds of trouble billowing on the horizon.

And yet he stayed at the hotel.

Slocum tried to figure out why. Harriet Griffith was an attractive woman, but the promise of mere sex wasn't enough to make him risk his life as he was doing. Slocum didn't think of himself as a greedy or foolish man. The money from the opium den might be gone. Sheree Dupree might have stolen it from Beaumont.

Slocum decided not knowing what was going to happen drew him the most. Flirting with danger excited him strangely. The added fillips of the money and Harriet's charms added to the thrill. He smiled slowly as he looked out across the Del Monte Hotel's grounds.

He could learn to live like this all the time. But he knew it wasn't in the cards. If he didn't sample this lifestyle now, he might never do it.

A knock at his door caused him to spin, hand on his Colt Navy. He relaxed a mite when he saw Harriet slipping into his shadow-shrouded room.

"Are you decent?" she asked, looking around the room and not seeing him on the balcony.

"Sometimes. Other times I'm damned good."

"John!" she exclaimed. "You gave me a fright. I didn't expect you to be outside." Harriet came to stand beside him on the balcony.

"I wanted to ask you if you wanted to take a ride with that saloon whore."

"Sheree?" Slocum was surprised. "What are you saying?"

"I arranged a carriage ride around the grounds with her and Thorvald. I don't know why I did it," Harriet said. "You like her that much?"

"I don't care spit about her. She's got something of mine." Slocum saw the light in Harriet's eyes brighten. He also saw how she began ruminating on this. It wouldn't take a clever woman like her long to figure out what a saloon girl like Sheree Dupree and John Slocum had in common.

Her quickness at finding the answer startled Slocum.

"Joshua Beaumont," she said with conviction. "He always had low tastes. He met her in the Slaughterhouse Saloon and gave her something—and you want it."

"Tell me about Beaumont," urged Slocum, wanting to get her talking about something other than Sheree.

"She doesn't have it," Harriet said with conviction. "Eleanore has it. Sheree is too frightened to ever do anything on her own. I don't know why Eleanore allowed her to come to this gala."

Slocum wasn't interested in how the madam picked her flock to keep the rich men from San Francisco high society happy. All he wanted was the stolen money. "I need to talk to Sheree for just a few minutes. You're coming along on this ride with her and Thorvald?"

"Naturally," Harriet said, as if he had asked the stupidest question in the world. He saw that she wasn't likely to trust him alone with the other woman, even with Thorvald along.

Slocum and the blonde joined the other couple in the lobby. Max Thorvald looked angry at the intrusion into his life. He glowered at Slocum, as if accusing him of some major crime. Slocum decided his truculence was permanent and nothing had been done to cause such a reaction.

"Let's get this over with," Thorvald said.

"Max my darling, this is a relaxing sojourn, not a contest to be run as quickly as possible," said Harriet.

"I'm not your darling," he said, but Slocum saw the way he eyed the lovely blonde. Thorvald considered exchanging his catch for Harriet Griffith.

It pained Slocum to do it, but he pushed Harriet toward the man with a shove of his elbow. This allowed him to sidle up to Sheree.

"Have we met?" the woman asked. Her brown hair had been caught up in a flurry of pearls and netting. Slocum didn't think the pearls belonged to the saloon girl. Her words came out harsher than Harriet's, and her manners weren't nearly as good.

"No," Slocum said, "but I'd like to get to know you better." He offered her his arm. She paused for a moment, then realized she ought to take it. Sheree smiled broadly as Slocum escorted her from the lobby. An open carriage and driver waited patiently for them.

"Take us around the grounds," ordered Thorvald. He glared at Slocum. Whatever Harriet had said to the shipping magnate didn't sit well. He shoved Slocum out of the way to sit beside Sheree in the carriage.

"We have a mutual friend," Slocum said. He didn't have time to sweet-talk the information he needed from Sheree

Dupree. A straightforward request might work better than being subtle. "Joshua Beaumont."

"Him?" snorted Thorvald. "A poor loser if ever I saw one. The man can't play cards worth shit."

"He has never failed to pay his debts," Slocum said, guessing that Beaumont had robbed other opium dens to finance his poor cardplaying. "Joshua was always an honorable man—in this regard."

Thorvald did not want to be in the open carriage. He took out his ire on Slocum. "The hell you say," Thorvald shouted. "He owes me a hell of a lot of money. If ever I find his worthless carcass, I'll take it out in flesh."

"He was shanghaied," Slocum said. "By your crimps." The last was a guess on Slocum's part. If Thorvald had as many China clippers as Harriet claimed, he needed crew members constantly. It made sense that he sent out crimps to keep his ships' complements intact.

"Prove it," the shipping magnate shot back. The scar across Thorvald's pocked face glowed in the blood-red light cast by the last rays of the sun.

"We both know," Slocum said easily. He shifted in the carriage seat to be sure he could reach his pistol if the need arose. Thorvald wasn't tall, but he was sturdy. From the play of the cloth, Slocum guessed real muscles lay beneath the finery—and that Max Thorvald had a nasty streak in him a mile wide.

Thorvald started to rise, but Sheree held him down. The man grumbled but didn't make any further fuss. He motioned to the driver to start. The carriage took off with a lurch that pushed Slocum back in the deep cushions. He watched the scenery unfolding around him with half an eye. Thorvald and the danger he presented bothered Slocum more than the woodlands and ocean soothed.

Harriet and Sheree chattered on endlessly about trivial

matters. Slocum soon realized he was in a staring match with Thorvald. The man's cold, flinty eyes never strayed from Slocum's equally cold green ones.

"What makes you so special you get an invitation to the Del Monte Hotel?" the shipping magnate finally asked when he realized he couldn't outstare Slocum.

"Investments," Slocum said easily. "Usually around a poker table."

Thorvald cleared his throat. "A damned parasite, a gambler. Men like you live off the sweat of others."

"Like you?" Slocum held his anger in check. Thorvald had crimps working to supply his ships with unwilling crews. He had read it in the man's face. Nothing struck Slocum as worse than such slavery.

"I work for my money. Nobody gives me nothing."

"This is Pebble Beach," Harriet cut in, trying to forestall a fight. "Isn't it lovely?"

"Stop the carriage," ordered Thorvald. "Me and this gent have something to settle."

Slocum got out, not knowing what to expect. Thorvald moved well, his motions quick and assured. Slocum didn't know if he wanted to have a bare-fist brawl with the shipowner. The six-shooter resting in his belt might prove a better solution.

He knew that any chance of recovering the money Beaumont had stolen would be lost if he killed Thorvald. Slocum shrugged it off. Staying alive was more important than all the money from all the San Francisco opium dens.

"Max, what are you doing?" asked Sheree. Slocum couldn't tell if she was more afraid of the man's violent nature or the possibility that he might end up dead. Losing her meal ticket at the Del Monte Hotel would cost her lucrative future jobs with Eleanore Lexington.

"Don't worry. I just want to see what kind of man this

gambler is," Thorvald said. He shucked off his expensive coat and tossed it on the ground. "Let's go a round or two." He doubled his fists and waited for Slocum.

"Why? I only fight if I have a reason."

"You candy-assed son of a bitch. Come on and fight." Thorvald hopped closer and took a swing at Slocum. Slocum ducked and sidestepped, letting Thorvald go past. He had the chance to end the fight then and there—but he didn't want the shipping magnate's death on his hands. There were too many witnesses.

"I don't fight because some fool calls me names," Slocum said. "I prefer to have something to win."

"Name your stakes." Thorvald wanted to fight. "Any amount you come up with I'll match."

"Her," Slocum said.

"What?" Thorvald stopped. He lowered his fists for a moment and stared as if Slocum had made a bad joke. "You want *her*?"

"If I win, you walk back to the hotel and the ladies both stay with me."

"That's *all* you want to wager? You walk back if I win? And I get the pair of them for the night?"

"John!" Harriet was outraged. "I'll have no part of this."

"Shut up, bitch. I know who pays you—and for what." A broad smile crossed Thorvald's face. "I like it. And you ain't gonna be in any condition to walk when I'm done with you."

Slocum didn't even bother taking off his jacket. He had seen barroom fighters like Thorvald before and knew their weaknesses. They used strength instead of brains. If they didn't overpower their opponent quickly, they were lost.

Slocum let Thorvald make the first move. The haymaker would have felled a giant, had it landed. Slocum ducked and felt the force of the fist's passage past his cheek. He bobbed again and avoided a second huge swing coming from the opposite direction. Thorvald had himself spun around, arms crossing his body. Slocum drove two quick blows into the man's upper arms. Neither did much damage, but Slocum knew the eventual effect: Thorvald would find his strength fading as bruises formed.

Slocum took a few hard blows to the body. He rode them the best he could and kept working on Thorvald's upper arms. The combination of the shipping magnate's exertion as he threw all his energy into every punch and the solid blows to his biceps started to take a toll. Slocum saw how Thorvald's guard began dropping.

He measured his distance, waited, and struck. A solid punch to the chin took Thorvald out. Slocum cursed, his fingers smarting from the impact against the man's jawbone. He hoped he hadn't broken any bones in his hand, but the blow had been necessary.

"Let's go," he said to the driver as he got into the carriage.

"We can't just leave him lying in the middle of a field," the driver protested.

"You heard the bet. He lost." Slocum's cold tone made the driver blanch.

"Yes, sir, whatever you say." He put the whip to the horse and drove for several minutes until they were out of sight of the sward where Thorvald lay unconscious.

Slocum settled into the seat beside Harriet, his eyes on Sheree. Her eyes were bright with a mixture of fear and anticipation.

"You fought for me," she said in wonder. "What do you want us to do? I never done anything like this before."

"I haven't either. And I won't," declared Harriet.

"Wait here for a few minutes," Slocum told Harriet.

"You want me to get out? Walk back?"

"We'll be back within five minutes. Stay here with the carriage," he said. He grabbed Sheree's hand and pulled her from the carriage. Harriet started to protest, then subsided. Her anger was like a raging fire. Slocum felt it on his back as he walked out of earshot with Sheree.

"Here?" the saloon whore asked. "I reckon it's all right." She started to lift her skirts.

Slocum stopped her. "I don't want that from you. I want to learn everything about Beaumont."

"Beaumont?" Confusion crossed her face. Then she understood. "You mean Josh! What about him?"

"I know he gave you the money," Slocum bluffed. "What did you do for him?"

"What's this to you? Josh is a friend."

"A friend or another customer?" Slocum had no time to mince words.

"Both. He comes in all the time. He always treated me good. He's not like some of the others."

"The money," Slocum prodded. "Why did he give it to you? To keep the bag for him?"

"You know about that? Look, mister, this ain't right. If Josh had wanted me to tell, he would have said it was all right. He didn't."

"Beaumont is dead," he said brutally. From the fear in Sheree Dupree's eyes, Slocum knew she thought he had killed Beaumont. He did nothing to correct her mistaken conclusion.

"Don't hurt me. Eleanore said there wouldn't be anyone getting hurt here."

"I'm not going to hurt you if you tell me what you did with the bag."

"I did just like Josh told me. He . . . he gave me fifty dollars to be sure the bag got to Eleanore. And I gave it to her." Sheree almost sobbed now. "And I had to give her the greenback, too. She wouldn't let me keep it. She said I work for her and that was part of what I owe her. The bitch!"

Slocum had no sympathy for her. He guessed that Beaumont had given her more. Perhaps he had given her two fifties, one of which had ended up in Eleanore Lexington's coffers.

"Did you look in the bag?"

"No. Josh said it was important to get the bag to Eleanore. He said he owed her."

Slocum sighed. The money might be gone. Beaumont might have been paying off a debt to the madam.

"She brought it with her," Sheree said.

"What? What do you mean?" Slocum's irritation vanished.

"The bag. Eleanore has it. The lock's still on it. I don't know if she opened it. She might be waiting for Josh. She always did have a yen for him." Sheree pouted. "And he liked her more'n he did me, too."

The picture he got of Joshua Beaumont changed constantly. Profligate, a womanizer, Beaumont got around San Francisco society—and its underbelly.

"Where does she keep it?"

Sheree shook her head. "I don't know. I don't much care. I got my money." She stared at Slocum with wide eyes. "He's really dead?" The tears that formed looked real to Slocum. She might have cared for Beaumont in her own way. For all he knew, Beaumont might have cared for Sheree Dupree.

Getting a look inside the bag Eleanore Lexington had

received from Beaumont would tell him if he was on a wild good chase or had hit the mother lode. But how was he going to do this bit of legerdemain? Slocum didn't know, but he'd find a way.

His nose itched with the smell of the stolen money.

9

Slocum couldn't sleep. He paced back and forth in his lavish room, occasionally going out on the balcony and watching the frantic activity on the well-kept lawn below. Although it was past midnight, the workers were toiling to erect huge gas lamps and walls of mirrors. Slocum chafed at having to stay in his room. He wanted to drop by Eleanore Lexington's room and search for Beaumont's bag filled with money. But being caught roaming around the Del Monte Hotel now might mean immediate expulsion—or worse.

He had returned with Sheree and Harriet the previous evening. Harriet refused to speak with him because of his short sojourn with the other woman. For his part, he didn't care to engage in polite conversation or anything else. He thought too hard about all Sheree had told him.

Of Max Thorvald he saw nothing. The shipping magnate had had more than his chin bruised. Slocum didn't want to cross a proud and spiteful man who had been knocked out in front of two women and a carriage driver. Such an affront could be met only with blood.

Slocum smiled at this. Thorvald wasn't likely to find him unless he incautiously poked around the hotel. The room was registered in Jakey Leonard's name. Even a shipping magnate would think twice about banging on the

San Francisco assistant police commissioner's door and demanding a rematch at fisticuffs.

He leaned against the wrought-iron railing and watched as a few workers tried out the strange contraption they were assembling. Slocum shielded his eyes as sudden brightness flared in his face. The gas lamps shone brightly into the mirrors. The curving wall of mirrors reflected the full light onto the hotel's front and turned it into a shimmering palace like ones Slocum had seen in books from Europe.

He left the balcony and fell heavily onto the soft bed. He lay staring at the ceiling for what seemed hours. The rattle of carry-alls and tallyhos awoke him long after sunrise.

He returned to the balcony and saw empty carriages coming around the corner of the hotel. He realized that the opening day had come and the train from San Francisco laden with dignitaries had arrived. Slocum heaved a sigh. Should he leave in the confusion of the gala and save his neck or should he try to fetch the money bag from Charles Crocker's madam?

Prudence dictated a quick flight, but instead he dressed for the tour of the Del Monte Hotel.

The huge lobby had already filled with the well-dressed revelers from San Francisco. A loud rapping got their attention. Quiet fell over the crowd as a portly man stepped onto a dais erected at the far end of the extravagant room. One hand hanging onto his left lapel in the manner preferred by orators, the other waving grandly, Charles Crocker welcomed his guests to the Del Monte Hotel.

Slocum paid scant attention to the railroad magnate's exuberant words. He wanted to find Eleanore Lexington or even Harriet. He didn't know what the madam looked like. And he didn't see Harriet anywhere in the crowd to ask her.

When the Del Monte tour began, Slocum kept to the rear of the crowd. He had spotted Max Thorvald and Sheree Dupree. Thorvald spoke intimately with Crocker and another man Slocum thought he recognized as Collis Huntington. Thorvald traveled in rich company.

What worried Slocum even more than running afoul of Thorvald was the presence of so many Oriental servants. The tong knew he was alive. Could the On Leong tong—or Fah Lu—reach down the peninsula to Monterey and find him?

"A thousand dollars," he muttered to himself. "That opium den had to have that much. Maybe more. Beaumont had hinted at twice that."

"How's that, sir?" asked a servant behind Slocum. "Is there anything I can get for you?"

"Nothing. Just talking to myself." Slocum silently cursed his own folly. Speaking aloud when others could overhear was a bad habit. This time he had been lucky. It might have meant his death in other circumstances.

Slocum spent the remainder of the day making himself inconspicuous in the throng of well-heeled people. At one time he estimated more than a thousand had come for the opening of Crocker's fabulous hotel. That night he changed into his other suit of clothes and went into the main ballroom. Once more the silent presence of so many Celestials bothered him. Then he forgot about them and lost himself in the mad whirl of high society. For a man used to roaming the mountains and plains, this was a major change in companionship.

"Harriet!" he called when he saw the stunning blonde woman. "Can I speak with you?"

She turned cold blue eyes on him and spun on her heel.

She stalked off without a word. Two men behind him exchanged whispers concerning her behavior—and its probable cause. Slocum ignored them and followed her across the dance floor. He deftly avoided dancing couples but fell far behind the fleeing woman.

By the time he reached the far side. Harriet was speaking in guarded tones with an older woman. A few strands of gray hair dotted an otherwise jet-black coiffure, but Slocum saw that the woman wasn't very old. She might not even be older than he was. She carried herself with a rigid dignity that fit in perfectly with the people gathered in the Del Monte Hotel's ballroom.

He didn't have to be told this was Eleanore Lexington. Her eyes darted here and there, studying, appraising, making decisions, and categorizing everyone she saw. Slocum doubted that very much went on in San Francisco that she didn't learn about first.

From her efficient system of soiled doves fluttering around the rich and powerful of San Francisco, she might know more than ever became public knowledge.

Harriet saw Slocum coming and stuck her nose high into the air. She stormed off without waiting for him.

"Good evening, Mr. . . . Leonard," Eleanore greeted him.

"Miss Lexington. A pleasure to make your acquaintance. May I have a word with you?"

"Of course, sir, but later. In one hour. On the terrace. They are turning off those terrible gas lamps soon. The area will be more . . . discreet." She smiled graciously and waved her fan in the direction of a portly man bedecked in diamond studs and ruby rings. She bowed slightly in Slocum's direction and glided away to talk with the bejeweled man.

Slocum wondered what Harriet had told her. Eleanore

Lexington, of all people, knew he wasn't the Assistant Police Commissioner. Why she chose to go along with his charade was something he would have to find out later.

He knew she wasn't expecting to meet with him for an hour. That gave him plenty of time to enter her room and search for Beaumont's money-filled bag.

Slocum slipped from the ballroom undetected. He waited for two passing waiters to vanish into the kitchens; he didn't trust any of the Celestial servants even though they had done nothing to alert him to danger.

The lights outside winked off as he wandered the hotel halls searching for Eleanore's room. She had been right about the gas lamps being turned off. He wondered if she was in charge of everything at the Del Monte Hotel. Charles Crocker didn't seem the type of man to tend to details. Those were the annoying little gnats best left to others for swatting.

"Pardon me," he said, stopping a bellman. "I have a note for Miss Lexington. Could you tell me what room she is in?"

"I can deliver the note, sir. I saw her in the main ballroom with Mr. Stanford a few minutes ago."

"This is a personal note. A *very* personal note. I want to slip it under her door myself." Slocum smiled and gave the bellman a broad wink. The bellman nodded. He understood. He pointed down the corridor and told Slocum where to find Eleanore Lexington's room.

It took Slocum less than a minute to jiggle the door handle and force the lock. He slid into the room and began searching. Fifteen minutes later he was angry. Beaumont's bag was nowhere to be seen. He even tapped the walls looking for secret compartments. He had found nothing. Nothing!

He ducked back into the corridor and immediately knew

he wasn't alone. He closed the door behind him quickly, turned, and rapped smartly on Eleanore Lexington's door, as if he had just come along. He knocked a second time then turned away, hoping that whoever was spying on him thought he was a rejected suitor.

As he turned the corner in the hall leading back to the ballroom, a hard fist landed in his belly. Slocum had a fraction-of-a-second warning. He grunted and tensed his belly in enough time to keep from being knocked out by the blow.

It still staggered him. He stumbled back against the wall, fighting for balance and breath. A second blow landed. He partially deflected it with his outthrust arm.

A second man joined the first in hammering at him. The man yelled in pain as one blow landed squarely on Slocum's hidden Colt Navy. The impact made him think ribs had broken—but his attacker's meaty hand was in even worse shape. This slight opening gave him the chance to lash out.

He shoved one man back. The second he knocked out with a hard fist to an exposed throat. The man gurgled and gagged, dropping to the floor. Slocum didn't know if he had killed him. He doubted it. He also doubted that the man would speak again. Cartilage in the Adam's apple had broken under his solid punch.

"You're gonna die for this," growled the first attacker. Slocum got a better look at him. He had the build of a crimp but wore fashionable evening clothes. The man might have been a secretary or valet to any of those dancing in the ballroom.

He didn't look as if he belonged in hotel corridors trying to waylay guests.

Slocum decided he didn't have to use his pistol. He weaved and dodged to one side and let the man's fist go past his head—and into the wall. The crunch of breaking plaster was drowned out by the man's shriek of agony.

Three hard blows to the man's exposed belly put him on the floor. Slocum measured the distance and kicked. His boot connected squarely with the point of the man's chin. Head snapping back, he wasn't likely to bother Slocum again.

The brief scuffle had gone unnoticed by any of the hotel staff. Slocum checked both men for wallets. Although they carried no identification, they both had thick wads of scrip. For his trouble Slocum took the greenbacks and replaced the emptied wallets in the men's inner coat pockets.

He had made almost two hundred dollars in less than a minute. And he still hadn't found the loot from Fah Lu's opium den.

Slocum returned to the ball. He had skinned the knuckles on his right hand. He looked around and found a long bar. Glancing behind it he found a small bucket filled with ice. He wondered if Crocker had brought it down from San Francisco or fetched it from the Sierras. It didn't matter. The coldness on his skin took the sting away. He flexed his fingers a few times and decided there wouldn't be any stiffness. If Thorvald found him—or the tong or the San Francisco police—he wanted to be able to use his gun hand unimpeded by injury.

"You handle yourself well, Mr. Leonard," came a cool voice. Slocum turned and saw Eleanore Lexington a few paces away. She had an amused expression on her face. "You are not the common road agent I mistook you for. My apologies."

"Road agent?" he asked. He saw a Chinese servant bending over a large wooden barrel filled with rubbish. The servant listened intently to the byplay.

"Again, please accept my apology. I misjudged you based on what one of my ladies said."

"Harriet Griffith?"

"It doesn't matter. Come, let's dance. You do dance?"

"I've been known to." Slocum took the elegant woman's arm and led her to the dance floor. It had been a spell since he'd danced with such a lovely woman in his arms, and it took a few bars before he fell into the rhythm. Then he danced easily and well.

Eleanore complimented him on his grace. "You continue to surprise me. Daring is often only foolishness. Why did you come to the Del Monte when it is so dangerous?"

"The food is superb," he said. "The hotel itself is the most beautiful I've ever seen—as are the ladies here."

"A fool and a gallant one, to boot," she said, laughing. They whirled across the floor. "Miss Griffith said you were a churlish brute. How is it she is so wrong?"

"She detected my true purpose for coming here," Slocum said, readying his lie. "I am seeking out counterfeit money and know that a business associate of yours received some."

"A business associate?" Eleanore asked. Her well-sculpted, plucked eyebrows rose the merest amount in disbelief. "Who might this be?"

"Sheree Dupree. She received it from Joshua Beaumont in a low dive along the Embarcadero in San Francisco."

"Sheree is involved in counterfeiting?" Eleanore tried not to laugh. "Really, sir. You are most amusing."

"Although I think she is an unwitting accomplice, it's true," Slocum said, warming to his lie. "She received the money and gave me to believe she passed it along to you."

"I have received money from many of my co-workers," she said, not forthrightly naming them. "It is the nature of my business."

"I'm not saying Miss Dupree—or you—had anything to do with counterfeiting. Receiving the fake money is not a crime. Concealing it after receiving it is."

"Will you exchange this money for legitimate scrip?" Eleanore appeared to have tired of the dance. The music played on, but she had stopped in the center of the parquet dance floor.

"I am authorized to do so," Slocum said. He hoped that she kept all her money in Beaumont's bag. Finding the money passed from Beaumont's hand to Sheree's would aid him in locating the money stolen from Fah Lu's opium den.

"Very well. Let's go to my room. I will give it to you in exchange for legitimate scrip."

Slocum followed her across the floor. Eyes followed them. Not a few of the men wondered at a stranger leaving with the famous—or infamous—Eleanore Lexington. Some envied him, more hated him for his privileged position.

Slocum rested his hand on the butt of his six-shooter as they passed the area where the two men had attacked him earlier. Both had vanished. Even the smears of blood on the wall had been neatly cleaned. No evidence of an altercation remained.

When Eleanore opened the door to her room, Slocum wasn't even surprised to see that the lock he had forced had been replaced. She paid no attention to the slight disarray he had left the room in after his search.

"I am always willing to cooperate," Eleanore said. Slocum watched as she went to the armoire and opened the front doors. He had searched inside and found nothing. He cursed to himself when he saw her reach inside and fumble for a secret catch. A tiny door opened in the side to reveal a hidden compartment. He had given the room walls a cursory examination for secret panels. There hadn't been time to carefully test the furniture, too.

"Here is the money Sheree gave me in San Francisco. I am sure it is what you are looking for, Mr. Leonard." The madam's inflection told him that she knew he wasn't the assistant police commissioner.

Slocum took the money—it was only a five-dollar greenback. Sheree had said she had received a fifty from Beaumont and had given it to Eleanore.

"Here is the replacement," he said, using one of the bills he had taken from his attackers. Slocum decided that the saloon whore had lied to him. Fifty dollars sounded as if Beaumont trusted her, that she was important and worth such a princely sum. It was far more likely that Beaumont had given her only a five.

Eleanore Lexington laughed and handed back his money. "Keep it. You need this more than I."

Slocum said nothing. He felt the tension in the room mounting.

"Keep the greenback and go with my promise that I won't tell Mr. Crocker about you, Mr. Slocum. Don't look so shocked. You couldn't possibly believe I mistook you for Jakey Leonard. As far as the assistant police commissioner is concerned, I'm happy he is dead. The man was a dishonest crook—he didn't stay bribed."

"The men in the hall. You sent them after me?"

"Harriet was worried about my safety. They're my bodyguards. You handled them nicely, sir. I wish I had more time to find out what it is that you're after. Alas, I do not. Mr. Crocker has commissioned me handsomely to see to the opening of the Del Monte Hotel. He's calling it the Queen of the American Watering Places. The man has little tact and thinks this hideous appellation will draw people."

"The hotel is beautiful."

"*That* will draw them from San Francisco and even Europe. Not some bizarre catchphrase." She opened her fan and stared at Slocum over the rim. "I must return to the ballroom."

Slocum opened the door for her. Eleanore Lexington slipped past and walked down the corridor, head high and shoulders back. She carried herself like royalty, Slocum thought. And she controlled every detail in the hotel's grand opening.

He had been dismissed, told to be on his way. He closed the door to the woman's room and returned to his own. Eleanore hadn't even bothered to see if he left or stayed to search. She knew he would find nothing—not then and certainly not before, when he had broken in.

Slocum had hard decisions to make. Without Eleanore Lexington's tacit support he could not survive a minute at the hotel. And he had been summarily dismissed by the madam.

10

John Slocum returned to his room and sat in a chair by the door, lost in thought. He pulled out the five-dollar bill Eleanore Lexington had given him. Which woman had lied? Sheree had said she had given her employer a fifty. Eleanore had claimed it was only a five—and that this bill was it. Slocum hadn't bothered asking about the bag Sheree claimed was in Eleanore's possession.

Slocum folded and refolded the five-dollar greenback. Eleanore didn't have to give him anything. She had seemed almost contemptuous that the bill was only five dollars. It had also put the lie to his fabricated story about tracking down a counterfeit bill. Who counterfeited a five when they could make a fifty for the same amount of work?

Sheree was lying, Slocum decided. The saloon whore might have received a fifty and passed along a five to Eleanore. That seemed most likely to Slocum. But who had the bag filled with Beaumont's money? If not Sheree or Eleanore, then who had it?

Slocum heaved himself to his feet and walked to the balcony. On the lawn below leading down to the bay milled many of the gala's guests. Here and there among them were the painted women Eleanore Lexington had recruited. Slocum wondered what secrets they learned and passed along to their employer—and how would Eleanore Lexington use that information?

His chances for recovering the money from Fah Lu's opium den were diminishing by the second. As he stared out over the revelers, he saw Max Thorvald and Charles Crocker. The pair strolled along, lost in private conversation. This worried Slocum. That Thorvald was a guest meant nothing. Anyone who owned more than a pair of shoes had been invited to the Del Monte Hotel's grand opening. The way the two men spoke when they were together meant they were friends and possibly even business partners.

Slocum knew he was surrounded by tong, by Eleanore's bodyguards, by Thorvald's anger at having his jaw knocked about by a mere gambler. Even worse, some of the guests had connections with the San Francisco Police Department. They would soon be asking where the assistant police commissioner was. When one of the staff pointed him out and Slocum didn't look anything like their swinish Jakey Leonard, nooses would be knotted and vigilante posses formed.

The money in his pocket made a nice wad. He hadn't been left penniless by his bad luck. Leonard had given up a few dollars. Eleanore's bodyguards a few more. He had enough to make his way to the Southern Pacific Railroad station and get back to San Francisco or ride the rails to anywhere he wanted to go.

Curiosity started to gnaw at him, even more than greed did. What *had* happened to Beaumont's bag?

Slocum smoothed the wrinkles in his coat and made sure his Colt rode easy at his side. He had to return to the ball and find the answers to his questions. If he didn't, he would go to his grave worrying over the answers.

He smiled ruefully. He might go to his grave all the sooner for trying to find out.

The crush in the ballroom had grown worse. Everyone wanted to dance. Even the immense floor was not able to accommodate more than three hundred couples at a time. Slocum drifted along the walls, his keen eyes seeking others in the crowd who might come after him or who might help him. He didn't see Eleanore Lexington. Her business had taken her elsewhere, he supposed. Crocker, Thorvald, and the other railroad magnates were outside indulging themselves in the luxury of the night breezes blowing across the neatly kept lawns.

When he saw Sheree by herself, he pushed through the throng and went to her.

"You," she said. "I didn't think you were staying. Miss Lexington said—"

"I don't care what she said. You were lying."

Sheree looked around. She reminded Slocum of a fawn trapped by a predator and vainly seeking some escape.

He grabbed her arm just as she bolted. "Where is the bag? The one Beaumont had. Eleanore doesn't have it. And I believe her."

"I . . . I just said that because you wanted to hear it," the saloon whore said. "You seemed like a nice man—and you had knocked out Max. I wanted to please you however I could."

"Where is the bag?"

"I don't know. Josh mumbled something about it, but he was in a bad way."

"What do you mean?"

"His wound. He was bleeding. I took him into the cribs and patched him up the best I could. I used both my petticoats doing it. He gave me the money to pay for them."

"You're still lying," Slocum said harshly.

"No!"

Sheree jerked away and dodged through the crowd. Slocum took off after her. A few men glared at him, but he didn't care. The woman lied every time she opened her mouth. He had to get to the truth if he ever wanted to find the money stolen from Fah Lu's opium den. Beaumont might have been injured. It explained his inability to fight off the crimps when they shanghaied him.

"John!"

He looked over his shoulder. Harriet was hurrying toward him, her elegant painted wood fan fluttering wildly as she walked. He saw how she used it to clear a path for herself. Men and women alike backed off as the fan sliced and slashed at them.

He stopped, watching Sheree vanish through a set of French doors onto the veranda. She would go find Max Thorvald. Talking to her after that would be impossible—and even deadly.

"John, don't go. I want to talk to you. I'm so sorry for the way I've acted."

"Harriet, I'm busy."

"John," she said, her eyes peering over the edge of the fan in a coy fashion. He heaved a sigh. His chance at questioning Sheree had not gone well. Now he had to deal with Harriet Griffith.

He began to regret his decision not to leave the Del Monte Hotel and find refuge somewhere deep in the Sierra Madres. Society and its trappings were not for him.

"Don't be angry with me. I want to make it up to you. I know now that you and the . . . woman didn't do anything when you left me in the carriage. You couldn't. You weren't gone long enough. And I know firsthand how *thorough* you are."

"She has something I want," he said. "I told you that before, and you didn't believe me."

"I talked to Eleanore. She told me what went on with you and Sheree."

Slocum was skeptical about that. He thought that Harriet had come to the conclusion that he hadn't really done anything by another route. He wanted to find Sheree but knew he had lost his chance.

"Let's dance." She took his hand and pulled him toward the floor. The waltz swelled and flowed, and Slocum found himself forgetting about the money and Eleanore and his troubles. He held Harriet close and danced as if they were the only two in the world.

When the music finished, he led her out to the veranda. He didn't see Sheree. Nor did he see Thorvald or Crocker or any of the railroad directors.

Slocum didn't know if he had wanted to see them. His world had changed when Harriet reentered it. Hand in hand they walked to the edge of the cliff looking down into the bay. Whitecaps appeared on the Pacific, and the waves beat relentlessly against the rocky shore. The soft warm breeze brought the scent of pine to his nose.

This was where he belonged, not inside with San Francisco high society.

"Let's go back," Harriet urged. "I want to make it up to you. I want to show you that I've forgiven you for the terrible thing you did with Sheree."

"I didn't do anything with her. I just wanted to be alone for a few minutes."

"*That's* the terrible thing," Harriet said, her eyes glowing in the darkness. "I want you all for myself. I know that's selfish, but I want it. John, you're different from the others. I know you're not rich, but that doesn't matter.

You're different. You're better than they are. You're the real man."

"Money changes you," he said. "It helps you, if you have enough."

"It changes you, but it's not necessarily for the better. Those men have all the money in the world, and what do they want? More!"

Slocum shrugged. He'd never had a fraction of the money those attending the Del Monte Hotel's grand opening carried loose in their pockets. And it didn't much matter. He usually had enough to get by, and that was good enough.

"Let's go back in. To your room," Harriet urged.

He shook his head. He thought of Eleanore's bodyguards, of the Chinese servants, of San Francisco police and everyone else after his scalp. Getting caught in bed with Harriet might shorten his life considerably.

"There," he said, pointing to a curving path going down the cliff to the beach below. He pulled her along. The blond followed reluctantly. She muttered to herself as the rocks worked against her high-heeled shoes and she almost turned her ankle. Slocum didn't mind giving Harriet the support she needed to traverse the narrow path.

When they got to the bottom of the cliff, they both agreed the walk had been worth the effort. The high rocky walls enclosed the tiny bay and shut out the rest of the world. The noise from the Del Monte was muffled and distant. Slocum closed his eyes for a moment and let the pounding surf totally erase the sound.

"It's wonderful here, John. Because I'm with you, it's even more wonderful," she said.

They walked along the sandy strip until Harriet pulled free. "Let me get my shoes off. Walking is so hard here."

Slocum looked up the cliffs and saw heads moving at

the very top. He and Harriet were the only ones daring enough to descend to the ocean. It suited him fine. For a brief time he could forget the danger that awaited him in the posh setting on the overlook.

He turned and looked at the woman working off her high-buttoned shoes. A daring amount of ankle showed as she worked off the balky shoes.

"Why stop there?" he asked.

Harriet jerked around and stared up at him. For a moment she didn't say anything. A slow smile spread across her face. Then she said, "That sounds like a good idea. Help me?"

Two steps took him to her, but he didn't get the chance to begin unfastening her dress. Not yet. Harriet eagerly began to work at his vest. The brocaded front pulled away, and she fumbled at his belt. He took the Colt out and laid it on the sand on top of his coat to keep the mechanism from getting jammed. By the time he had finished, Harriet had opened his trousers and fumbled around inside.

He gasped when she found the object of her search.

"Look at what I've found washed up on the beach. Can this be a sea shell?" she asked impishly. "Or it is something else? A mussel, perhaps?"

She pulled his length from the confines of his tight trousers and gently held it for a moment. Slocum moaned softly when she began sucking the tip. "Ummm," Harriet said around the fleshy plug in her mouth. "This is *good*."

He ran his hands through her blonde hair, guiding her head back and forth in a motion that set fire to his loins. He hardened until his erection pulsed painfully.

"I want you," he said, pulling free of the blonde's mouth. He sank down beside her. It took a few minutes to open her dress. The complicated fastenings almost eluded both of them. Harriet reached the point of jerking hard at the buttons and hooks. In her haste she ripped several out.

Slocum would have ripped her dress off to get to the firm white breasts that gleamed whitely in the soft moonlight. He kissed and fondled her breasts until the pink nipples stood out stiffly. He cupped the twin mounds of flesh and squeezed hard.

Harriet moaned and threw her arms around his neck. "I can't get enough of you," she said. Burying her face in his shoulder, she licked and kissed and sobbed softly.

"What's wrong?" he asked when he felt the hot tears on his naked flesh.

"Nothing. You're so different from them. You are, John."

Slocum didn't answer. He wasn't that distinctive. He had killed, sometimes in self-defense, and during the war he had ridden with Quantrill's Raiders and killed indiscriminately. What the men in the hotel did for money he had done out of patriotism. He wasn't sure if that made him any better than they were—or any worse.

He kissed her hard on the lips. They sank to the beach. Their hands explored one another's body, and they wiggled about until they were naked under the moon. Slocum wondered briefly what people on top of the cliff would see if they looked down and saw him and Harriet.

Then it didn't matter.

The woman's hand circled his throbbing length and pulled him firmly into her.

"Now, John. I want you now. Don't tease. Give it to me. I have to have it now!"

He felt the sand crunching under his knees as he positioned himself. The blonde's legs parted and exposed the dewy triangle of soft fur between her well-fleshed thighs. He scooted forward, bent, and lightly nipped at her snowy breasts, then licked his way up to her swanlike throat.

When their mouths again touched, he levered his hips forward and found his target.

Harriet gasped at the sudden intrusion into her most intimate territory. She lifted her legs and circled his waist to keep him from leaving. This was the last thing in the world Slocum wanted. He felt her excitement all around his hidden shaft and reveled in it. Let the others drink and party at the hotel. He had found his own special entertainment—and it was infinitely better.

He began pulling out slowly, teasing Harriet with every movement. When only the thick head of his cock remained inside her, he shoved back in. She gasped once more. This time she shoved her hips down to meet his. Hips grinding, she rotated her crotch to achieve the maximum stimulation.

Slocum felt his balls tightening. The fiery tide rose within him. He controlled himself. This time. The passionate woman's sobs and cries of joy tore at him even as she gripped down hard on his impaling lance of hot flesh.

"Don't stop, John. Never. Not ever. I can stay like this forever. I want to!" She bucked up and down and twisted around to get the most from the position.

He withdrew. For a few seconds he thought something had gone wrong. Wetness flooded his legs and body. He rose and saw that the tide had moved ever closer while he had been occupied by Harriet.

"The water," the woman gasped out. "The tide's coming in."

"Good," he said. They continued the slow back-and-forth motion as the water rose around their questing bodies. Slocum felt as if he was floating on a sea of desire. The water washed his body and erased all sensation but that building inside him.

Harriet clutched wildly at him and pulled herself up. A hot flush climbed from her breasts to her shoulders and finally past her neck to her face. She panted harshly. Her breasts heaved with reaction. She clawed at his back and went berserk around him.

He continued his deliberate motion as long as he could. The ocean lapped at his body even as Harriet tore at his flesh and tried to pull him ever deeper into her heated interior.

Slocum's control faded as desire mounted. His own body responded like the ocean's waves. Hot tides built within him until he could no longer contain them. They washed out and lapped at the inner shores of the woman's grasping hollowness.

He grunted as he spilled his seed into her. Even as he erupted, the tide washed over them. Slocum experienced a giddy moment when he thought they would turn as light as thistle and float away on the departing tide of water.

Sinking atop her, they lay spent for several seconds. The new rush of water brought them up to a sitting position, sputtering and wiping the water from their eyes.

"We were here longer than I thought," Harriet said. "Or we thrashed around until we got into the water."

Slocum blinked the last of the water from his eyes and studied the stars. "We've been down here for almost an hour. It's close to three in the morning."

Straining, he heard the band still playing at the Del Monte Hotel. The gala opening would go on for another day or more. He groped and found his coat and the pistol still above the tide. He didn't want to think about stripping the six-shooter to be sure the water hadn't worked its way into the firing mechanism and damaged it. Slocum relied on his Colt Navy. He had lost one. He should see about replacing it soon to have a spare when he needed it.

"Do we have to return to the hotel?" Harriet asked wistfully.

"You were the one who wanted to go to my room," he pointed out.

"I was wrong. You showed me something better." She grinned. He saw her strong white teeth in the moonlight. "Show me again. Even better, come and catch me!"

She got to her feet and ran into the surf, laughing and splashing like a young child.

Slocum watched her for a few seconds. Dark forms bobbed to the surface of the bay, then dived. He waited for them to surface again. He identified them as sea otters diving to find a meal on the bottom of the bay. They floated on their backs and used their bellies as a picnic table, tiny hands working on their food. When they finished, they lithely twisted and vanished from sight.

Harriet soon added a new dimension to their frolicking. Slocum saw no reason not to join her. He could worry about retrieving the lost money later.

11

"Drat," Harriet Griffith said when they reached the top of the cliff. She pointed toward the hotel veranda. Eleanore Lexington and three other women were standing outside. Eleanore was obviously giving them instructions that were not to their liking. It was equally obvious to Slocum that the women would do as they were told. Eleanore's stern manner brooked no disagreement.

"We were supposed to meet about now and find out what Eleanore wanted us to do the rest of the night." Harriet didn't have to tell him that she was skirting the real question. What Harriet and the others were to do with their time was obvious. With whom wasn't. Even at the Del Monte Hotel—or especially at the hotel—finding tidbits of interest to the madam took precedence.

"Go on," Slocum said. "Do what you have to."

"It's a bitch of a job," Harriet said. "I'm glad you understand. You're so different, John. Really." She stood on tiptoe and gave him a quick kiss. "I'll finish as soon as possible. Leave your room door unlocked."

The blond started to go, stopped, and looked back over her shoulder. An impish grin danced on her full, ruby lips. "I *enjoyed* our little dip in the Pacific." With that she hurried off.

Slocum had to admit he had enjoyed it too. Their

amorous antics in the ocean had frightened the feeding sea otters and a sea lion coming into the bay. He shook his head and got the last of the salt water from the lank black hair.

If Harriet had work to do, so did he. Staying another night at the Del Monte was out of the question. What he did had to be finished quickly. Too many people wanted him dead. It was only a matter of time before they found him and got their fondest wish.

Even though Harriet had distracted him, his mind had kept working at the problems presented by Sheree and the greenback Beaumont had given her. Eleanore Lexington had no reason to lie. She had even been amused at his audacity at asking for the bill. She hadn't believed his story of examining a possibly counterfeit piece of scrip. That had been proven when she had called him by his real name.

Not much slipped past the madam.

Slocum walked into the ballroom and saw that the band had finally stopped playing. Fewer than a dozen couples remained. A huge Regulator clock ticking solemnly at the far end of the room showed it to be almost five A.M.

Fingers of light were creeping up from the east, bringing the hint of a fine new summer day to the Monterey peninsula. Slocum had to be quick about his task or he wouldn't get a clue to where Joshua Beaumont had hidden the money.

He went to the registration desk in the lobby and, to his surprise, found a clerk on duty. He had hoped no one would be behind the polished mahogany desk. A few minutes' searching would have shown him where Max Thorvald's room was.

"May I help you?"

"I've an important message for Mr. Thorvald," he said.

"We can deliver it, sir."

"It has to be handed over personally. Business."

"Railroad business?" The clerk saw Slocum's frown and explained, "Mr. Thorvald is a director of the Southern Pacific Railroad. He and Mr. Crocker have numerous other business dealings. If it is business, perhaps Mr. Crocker can help you. I believe he is still awake. He just had coffee sent to his suite."

"This has to do with Mr. Thorvald's shipping concerns," Slocum said. "I can slide the letter under his door."

"Room 1009. That's in the western wing, sir. I assure you we can take care of this if you—"

Slocum was already on his way. Find Thorvald, find Sheree. The lying whore would tell him the truth this time. The whole truth. Every time she opened her mouth, she lied. He wanted to find out why, even though he knew this might just be her nature. Living a hand-to-mouth existence as a two-bit prostitute in the Slaughterhouse Saloon wasn't easy. Slocum didn't know if Beaumont had fixed her up with Eleanore or if that connection had come through other channels. However it was, becoming one of Eleanore Lexington's stable promised a better life than she was ever likely to get catering to drunken sailors on the Embarcadero.

The rooms along the hallway were either as silent as tombs or filled with boisterous sounds of late-night partygoers continuing their amorous revelry. Slocum stopped in front of Room 1009 and listened hard at the door.

He cursed. From the sounds inside, Thorvald wasn't anywhere near going to sleep. Slocum felt the pressure of time on him. If he didn't get the money stolen from Fah Lu soon, he would have to quit. No amount of money was worth his death.

Slocum left and went outside. In the shrubs he disturbed a portly man and one of Eleanore's ladies of the evening.

The woman wasn't upset. She looked Slocum over and winked broadly. The half-dressed man grunted and grumbled. Slocum moved on quickly, not wanting to raise a ruckus. He stopped outside the window he thought belonged to Thorvald. He tried counting from the corner of the wing-lobby junction and couldn't. The rooms didn't follow an exact numbering pattern.

When no one was in sight, Slocum stepped into the flower beds and pressed his ear against the windowpane. He heard nothing. He doubted Thorvald had finished yet, but he couldn't be certain. His fingers curled under the window. He lifted slowly. He thanked the careful planning and workmanship that had gone into building the Del Monte Hotel. There wasn't a hint of a squeak as the window slip upward easily.

Like a snake, he slithered over the ledge and into the room. He lay flat on the floor, letting his eyes adjust to the dimmer light inside. From the bed came heavy, deep breathing. Slocum rose up just enough to get a look at the sleeper's face.

He cursed. Whoever lay in the bed, it wasn't Max Thorvald. And the man was alone. Slocum worked his way back to the window and started to leave. Standing outside on the lawn were two Celestials. One turned and pointed to the window. Slocum caught a glint of light off a wicked butcher knife thrust at the man's sash. Both of the Chinese saw Slocum duck back down.

Slocum whipped out his six-shooter and made for the door leading into the hall. Those might not be tong killers after him. They might just be hotel employees who had seen him illicitly entering the room. Proving he wasn't a sneak thief would be hard. Proving he wasn't Jakey Leonard would be even easier when they questioned him. The fabric of his lies would come unraveled in no time.

"Get him," came the cry through the open window. Slocum heard the sound of feet hitting the carpet inside the room. He didn't know if those feet belonged to the room's occupant or the hotel's Chinese servants. It didn't matter. One was as bad as the other, as far as he was concerned.

He fumbled getting the door open. The man had locked it before going to bed. Slocum struggled to pull back the dead bold. A heavy *thunk*! sounded beside his head. A thick-bladed knife stuck in the door frame.

It had been the Celestial's footsteps he had heard.

Slocum ducked and spun, his pistol coming around. He didn't get a chance to fire. The barrel crashed into a grasping hand. He felt metal strike bone. The snapping sound marked breaking fingers. The noise following was another knife falling to the carpeted floor.

After that, Slocum wasn't sure what sound belonged to his assailant. Screams filled the room. The heavily sleeping man in the bed had finally come awake. He shouted and called for help. Slocum wasn't sure who he thought would come to his aid.

Pressed back against the door, Slocum fought for his life. The Celestial with the broken fingers managed to force the Colt Navy down toward the floor. Slocum fired. The Chinese yelped in pain. Slocum doubted he had severely injured the man; a simple wound gave enough of an opening for Slocum to shove him back. The man fell heavily.

Slocum dodged another projectile. A heavy hatchet sank into the hardwood door. If he'd had any doubt before about the identity of his attackers, this removed it. He faced tong killers. Hotel employees did not wander the grounds just before dawn carrying hatchets.

"What's going on? Get out, the lot of you. Out, you damned scoundrels!" cried the man in the bed. Slocum wrestled with the second tong assassin, struggling to keep hold of his six-shooter. To drop it now meant death.

He forced it around and brought it up between him and the Chinaman. When he thought he had a chance for a killing shot, he squeezed the trigger. The effort almost broke his finger. The normally loud report was muffled by the padded overcoat worn by the Celestial.

The man stiffened and fell backward, toppling like a felled tree.

"Robbers! Killers! Help me!" The man in the bed pulled the bedclothes up around his neck. Slocum wondered if the man thought the danger would go away if he couldn't see it. Whatever reasons the panicked man might have, they played into Slocum's hand.

He got the door open and erupted into the hall just as curious people in other rooms stuck their heads out.

"In there," Slocum shouted. "Two men tried to kill him. It's awful!"

Questions might have been asked if the surviving Chinese with the broken fingers hadn't followed into the corridor.

"Damn, the slant-eyed bastard is robbing us!" someone shouted. Gunfire erupted then—and it wasn't Slocum's doing. He hit the floor hard and wiggled away. Everyone who came into the hall had a weapon of some sort, and all used them.

Both Celestials were dead. One had fallen to Slocum's pistol. The other had been cut down with a variety of firearms. Of the man in the room, Slocum saw no trace. He doubted he had been hurt, but his sleep had certainly been interrupted.

Slocum walked back into the lobby, trying not to look out of place. Most of the men milling around were dressed for bed. One wore trousers hastily pulled on.

"Crocker's not going to cotton much to the idea of having thieves on his staff here," one man said. "I mean to give him a piece of my mind over this outrage. Sneak thieves! Imagine!"

Slocum waited for the commotion to die down. The efficient staff of the Del Monte quickly removed the dead Chinamen and soothed the ruffled nerves of the man in the room. They ended up showing him to another room.

And Slocum still had to talk to Sheree Dupree. It took more than a half hour before everyone was satisfied that the "thieving Chinee" had gotten their comeuppance and had returned to bed.

Slocum went back outside. This time he counted more carefully and located Thorvald's window. The window had been left open to capture as much of the ocean breeze as possible. He stuck his head in past the draperies and saw two sheet-shrouded forms on the bed. The one closer to the window was small. The other was bulky. From this he knew which was Sheree and which was Max Thorvald.

Something caused the woman to stir. She stretched, pushing the sheet off her. Slocum saw the flash of naked flesh in the increasing light of dawn.

She sat bolt upright in bed, her hand flying to her mouth.

"Quiet," whispered Slocum. He motioned for her to come to the window. Sheree glanced at the still sleeping Thorvald. The man's stentorian snores told that he had gone into heavy sleep and wasn't likely to awaken soon.

The woman got out of bed and found a robe. She pulled it around her thin body. "You shouldn't be here. Didn't you hear the commotion that went on a few minutes ago?"

Slocum didn't answer that. He had *caused* the furor. He motioned for her to leave through the window. She shook her head.

"Do it," he said, his words icy. "I don't want to talk here and wake him." He pointed at Thorvald.

Sheree shuddered. "He has quite a temper," she said, as if justifying her decision to leave. She pulled the robe even closer to her body and sat on the windowsill. Slocum helped her out into the cold morning Monterey air.

"What do you want?" she demanded once she was away from the room. Slocum grabbed her arm and dragged her toward a stand of trees at the edge of the cliff.

"You lied to me. I want to know why."

"I didn't!" she protested. She tried to bolt and run. Slocum was ready for her. He grabbed the lapels of her robe and lifted. In other circumstances he might have been interested in the show of female flesh as the belt came free. Not now. He wanted her to tell him the truth so he could get the hell away from the Del Monte Hotel.

He lifted her onto tiptoe until her face was only inches from his. "Beaumont gave you a fifty-dollar bill. Eleanore Lexington said you only passed along a five. I have it in my pocket."

"She's not telling the truth. I gave her the fifty!"

Slocum saw by her fear that Sheree was still lying.

"Where is the fifty Beaumont gave you?"

"I don't make much at the saloon. It's not much to someone like Miss Lexington. What's she care if she gets a five or a fifty? To me it means life or death!"

"You've still got the bill?"

"Yes! I haven't had time to spend it. Josh was always good to me. He arranged with Miss Lexington for this job. Don't take the money from me."

"You can keep the fifty if you tell me what happened to Beaumont's bag."

"I don't know anything about a bag. I lied before so you wouldn't hurt me. You wanted to hear something, and I kept talking until it looked as if you believed me."

Slocum relaxed his hold on her robe. Sheree sank to her knees in the dewy grass. He heaved a deep sigh. At last he believed her. She didn't know what Beaumont had done with the bag of money from Fah Lu's opium den. The only thing that made any sense to him was that there was a message written on the bill. Why else would Beaumont give a two-bit whore a fifty-dollar bill.

"He told you to give Eleanore Lexington the bill, didn't he?"

"Yes," Sheree sobbed. "I got flustered and told her about it. I wanted to keep it all, but she confuses me. She's a witch! She can see right through your soul. I hate her!"

"Beaumont told you to give the greenback to Eleanore. You gave her a five." In this Slocum saw a hint of intelligence in Sheree. A madam of Eleanore Lexington's standing wouldn't believe Beaumont had wanted her to have a mere dollar bill. A five was big money to someone like Sheree Dupree, and she thought it would be to Miss Lexington, too.

"Yes."

"I'll trade you a fifty for the one Beaumont gave you. You can identify the bill, can't you?"

She bobbed her head up and down. Slocum decided she wouldn't have any trouble finding the bill given her. How many fifty-dollar greenbacks would someone screwing sailors at a cheap dockside saloon for two bits have?

"Is it in the room?" he asked.

"Yes. It's in my purse. I don't want to go back there. Max is drunk. He beat me up."

Slocum lifted her chin and looked at her face. He didn't see any bruises. She silently pulled back and opened her robe to show dark spots forming around her thin breasts and along her flanks. Slocum said sourly, "Thorvald needs to be taught a lesson for this."

"You can do it. You knocked him out before."

"Did he say anything about it?"

"That's when he hit me with his belt. He's furious about what happened. He's been looking for you. I think he'd kill you if he found you."

"I don't doubt that. We'll take care of Thorvald later. Right now, go fetch the greenback Beaumont gave you."

"Can't we leave? I'll go anywhere with you. I . . . I'll do anything you want."

"The greenback," Slocum insisted. Although their circumstances were different, he couldn't help comparing Harriet and Sheree. Sheree was a pathetic little whore who would never escape the worst her profession had to offer. Harriet Griffith might work for Eleanore Lexington, but she retained a touch of dignity and style. Something more burned inextinguishably within her: pride.

Sheree Dupree—or whatever her name really was—would never have it and would always remain the victim.

"I'll get it. Then you'll keep him away from me?" The woman's plea was almost pathetic.

"I'll talk to Miss Lexington about it. She'll do something, I'm sure."

"Thank you," Sheree said. She got to her feet and chastely pulled her robe together. She fastened the belt and started back toward the open window of her room. Slocum stopped her.

A faint sound had come to his ears. Straining to hear, he waited for several seconds. All he heard was the soft whisper of wind through the tall pines and the cypress trees along the cliffs. Dawn cast golden rays across the Del Monte Hotel's lawn and turned the dew drops into tiny rainbows. The day was another fine one in Monterey. Slocum wished he could stay at the hotel and enjoy it.

After almost a minute of seeing nothing untoward, he pushed Sheree toward the hotel. She trotted away, her bare feet leaving outlines in the soft grass. Slocum's sixth sense still warned him of danger in the wind.

The woman reached the window and started to enter when Slocum saw movement at the corner of a topiary hedge. The lion shape turned into a man dressed in black padded coat and pants. The morning sun reflected off the wicked knife in the tong killer's hand.

"Sheree!" Slocum shouted.

Too late. The knife blazed a trail through the still air and sank between the woman's shoulder blades. She slumped to the ground without a sound.

Slocum knew he shouldn't have tried to give warning. The woman's fate was sealed before he had responded. The On Leong tong assassin spun, and a new knife appeared magically in his hand. This time Slocum was his target.

Slocum dodged behind a tree just as the shining cartwheel of death came through the air. The knife sank two inches into the tree trunk beside his head. Not stopping, Slocum dashed through the stand of trees, circling, hoping that he could get around his attacker.

The Celestial saw what Slocum intended and laid a trap for him. As Slocum came out on the rocky lip of the cliff, the tong killer exploded from behind a low shrub. A razor-sharp edge slashed at Slocum's eyes; he had faced enough knives in his life to know the trick. If he had reacted to this attack, another knife would have gutted him.

Slocum ducked under the knife intended to blind him even as he sought the wrist behind the second knife. He deflected the blow but felt a hot line along his chest as the sharp edge found his flesh. Slocum kept twisting. Groping wildly, he caught the wrist guiding the knife that had gashed him.

He fell and held on to his attacker. The tong killer yelped in surprise as he stumbled over Slocum's feet. The next instant he was tumbling through the air. Slocum came to hands and knees and watched as the killer crashed into the rocks seventy feet below. Given time, the tide would wash the body to sea.

All that mattered to Slocum right now was that he was still alive. Wincing, he put his hand to the cut on his side. His fine clothing had turned bloody, but a closer examination showed the wound to be shallow. He wasn't in any danger of bleeding to death from it.

Walking gingerly, he returned to the window. Sheree's death hadn't disturbed the sleeping Thorvald. The man was still snoring loudly.

Slocum looked around. No one had witnessed the woman's death. Grunting with pain, he hoisted her up and into the room. The oppressive smell of strong liquor told him that rather than sleeping Thorvald had passed out. No amount of noise would awaken him.

Slocum left Sheree on the floor under the window and went to search her purse. He found it under her clothing carelessly dumped at the foot of the bed. Sitting cross-legged on the floor, he rummaged through it until he found a small wallet. Inside he found a wad of greenbacks, mostly ones.

Carefully surrounded by the lower-denomination bills was a single fifty. Slocum stuck it into his shirt pocket. This was his only chance to find what Beaumont had done with Fah Lu's opium money.

Slocum looked at the now peaceful Sheree and then at Thorvald on the bed. He lifted the dead woman and dragged her to the bed. Careful not to disturb the knife protruding from her back, Slocum got her into bed with the shipping magnate.

Max Thorvald would have quite a surprise when he awoke.

"Confusion to my enemies," John Slocum said as he left through the window. He made sure his tracks were carefully obliterated in the flower bed and then went back to his room. He didn't have long before all hell broke loose at the Del Monte Hotel.

12

Slocum stopped in the lobby, knowing he would attract too much attention if he tried to go past the clerk at the registration desk. Even though it was only a few minutes past dawn, people were stirring in the lobby. Slocum would have bet that the late-night revelers would have slept till noon.

Too many guests were sauntering around for him to easily make it to his room. The wound on his side had bled and matted the shirt and jacket against his flesh. No matter how he held his arm, the cut jacket and the broad bloodstain would show. Attracting unwanted attention now meant death.

He looked around and tried to find some safer way to get to the stairs and his second-floor room. The only path open to him lay through the kitchens. He knew the servants had a back way to bring food to guests in the rooms without going through the public lobby.

This was almost as dangerous. Three tong killers had come after him. All three were dead—but how many more lurked around the hotel posing as servants?

Slocum had to take the chance. Explaining his problems to Charles Crocker would be more difficult than killing another On Leong assassin. Slocum hurried through the kitchen. The staff hardly looked up. He held his right arm close to his side, his hand resting on the ebony butt of his hidden Colt Navy. He wouldn't go hand-to-hand with anyone trying to stop him. This time his Colt would speak loudly.

He reminded himself that he had fired the pistol and had to reload. Not knowing how many cylinders remained unfired might mean the difference between life and death for him.

Slocum got to the back stairs and had to rest. He hadn't lost much blood, but the shock of the knife cutting through his body had taken something away from him. He had to sit down for a few minutes to recover his strength.

The sound of feet shuffling toward the door into the stairwell got him moving again. Through force of will he made it up the stairs and onto the second floor. He found his room and sank into a chair. He didn't think anyone had seen him.

He smiled wanly. Even if someone had, who was to say he wasn't a late-night carouser returning drunk to his room? Slocum wouldn't be the only man staggering around the hotel after the dance and all the free liquor being served at it.

He closed his eyes. He regretted not having spent more time at the dance. Free liquor. He counted the times he had wished for such a lagniappe. Crossing burning deserts, months spent in the snow-locked mountains, when he was down on his luck and didn't have two nickels to rub together, dozens of times he would have killed for a free sip of whiskey. And he had passed it by the night before.

He smiled more broadly as he remembered why he had ignored it. Harriet Griffith could make a man forget his thirst anytime. She fed a more basic hunger and did it well.

Slocum slipped off into a light sleep and came awake a half hour later with a start. Festivities at the hotel were getting under way. He heard the brassy strains of a band practicing before their concert. People came and went with increasing regularity along the hall. The Del Monte Hotel was becoming a beehive of activity once more.

Slocum knew he had to leave. The confusion of a band and the large lunch being prepared for the guests on the lawn would cover his retreat from Monterey.

He'd leave, that is, if he figured out where Joshua Beaumont had hidden the money they'd stolen. Slocum pulled the fifty-dollar bill from his shirt pocket and held it up to the light.

It didn't seem different from any other worthless piece of Union scrip he'd seen. Slocum preferred bright yellow metal for real money. A pair of twenty-dollar gold pieces meant more to him than this fifty-dollar piece of paper. Too many places discounted scrip. No one discounted cold, hard cash.

He examined the bill closely. It had to have come from Beaumont. The unfortunate Sheree wouldn't have earned it. She wouldn't have stolen it, either. Not from her class of patrons. The sailors fresh off the China clippers had pockets bulging with their pay for three months or longer, but not a one would have a fifty-dollar bill. Their earnings for the entire trip might not equal this much.

"Beaumont gave it to her," Slocum said aloud. "And she was supposed to pass it along to Eleanore Lexington. Why?"

The only reason he could think of was that the San Francisco madam would see something in the bill and know its significance. Beaumont had been pursued by the tong killers. Sheree had said he was injured and unable to run. And when he and Slocum had run afoul of the crimps, he hadn't had the bag.

"He hid it. The answer is in the bill." Slocum held it up

to the light and looked at it closely. Tiny brown smudges were all that made this bill any different.

"Bloodstains," he decided. "Beaumont's blood." Slocum scowled as he looked harder at the stains. They seemed too regular to be random discoloration. By using his imagination Slocum made out four numbers along the margin: 1723.

He had no idea what the numbers meant.

Heaving himself to his feet, Slocum went to the balcony and looked at the preparations for the continuing festivities. He wished he belonged here. The food was good, the company superb, and the amount of money being spent would keep him happily the rest of his life. A few well-chosen poker games with the railroad and shipping magnates would line his pockets with greenbacks for years to come. But staying presented more problems than abandoning his hunt for Beaumont's bag.

He spun when he heard someone rattling the brass doorknob at his room. His hand flashed to his ebony-handled Colt and he drew it, aiming directly for the woman's dark head thrust inside. The woman's eyes grew wide.

"Sorry," she said. "I . . . I just wanted to change the linens. I'm the maid."

"Later," Slocum said tiredly. "Come back later. When I'm out of the room." He lowered his pistol when her head vanished. He had given her a fright—but it wasn't anything like the one he had received.

Everyone was dangerous to him now. The Chinese servants. Crocker's men. Thorvald. Anyone knowing the real San Francisco assistant police commissioner. A trail of death had been cut behind him. Slocum tried not to think of the men and women who had died.

Beaumont and the other two trying to rob Fah Lu's opium den. Jakey Leonard. Three tong assassins. Sheree

Dupree. He didn't even consider the crimp he had slain. The man got what he deserved. The others were all tied directly to him, though.

Eight dead, half of them at his hand.

Slocum packed his meager belongings and prepared to leave the luxurious hotel. He was still in one piece, except for the cut on his side. He wanted to keep on keeping on for a long, long time.

Loud shouts came up from the lawn. Curious, Slocum stopped his packing and went to the balcony and looked over. Almost under his balcony stood Charles Crocker and Max Thorvald. The shipping magnate was shouting and waving his arms around like a windmill. No matter what Crocker said, it didn't soothe Thorvald.

". . . in my own bed. The damned whore got herself killed in my bed. What are you going to do about it, Crocker? What the hell kind of hotel is this you're running here? Killed right next to me, damn it! It could have been me!"

"You're taking this too personally, Max," Crocker said. "Whores like her have enemies all over the face of the earth. Sailors who think they're spurned. She might have—"

"She was killed by one of the tong, damn it. Don't you think I know a tong killing when I see it? I've dealt with those slanty-eyed bastards too much."

"I'm making inquiries among my staff," Crocker said, his voice turning colder. "I'm sure we'll get to the bottom of it. There are some other strange things happening."

"I heard. Three of your Chinee got themselves killed. Your Queen of the American Watering Places is going to get a reputation for having blood soaked into the carpets, Crocker."

"I've told Eleanore what happened. She's agreed that

Sheree Dupree will just . . . vanish. She's gone back to France, perhaps."

"France, my ass. She wasn't any French whore. All you had to do was listen when she opened her trap."

"Max, please. The body is being buried. We found a secluded spot over at Pebble Beach. No one asks any questions here that I don't want asked. She'll be forgotten in a week. In a month it'll be as if she never existed."

"Do you think *I* won't remember she got herself killed in *my* bed?"

"Calm yourself, Max. No one is going to know—or care."

Slocum almost called out in anger. These men were speaking of a woman's life as if it were nothing. The cold fire burning within him slowly died down. To them a life wasn't anything important. Crocker had engaged in dangerous chicanery to get the Monterey and Salinas Valley Railroad away from David Jacks. He wouldn't stop at murder, if it came to that. From all Slocum had seen, murder meant little to Max Thorvald, too.

"I want that man who rode with her in the carriage picked up," Thorvald went on. "He's the one I think did it."

"This was a tong killing, Max," Crocker said, trying to keep his business partner's voice down. "You just said so yourself. We found the other Chinese scattered around. There's something going on among them. We shouldn't poke around too much."

"Then you find the man in the carriage, blame him, and let the tong off the hook for the killing," Thorvald said. "I want him."

"He didn't break your jaw."

"He disgraced me in front of the women."

"The driver's been transferred back to San Francisco,"

Crocker said. "I look after my friends, Max. You know that."

"I want him."

"Max, you take all this too seriously. This is the Del Monte Hotel's grand opening. Relax. Enjoy yourself. I'm sure Eleanore has someone else who will suit you. Come along. Let's find her and ask."

The men walked away, oblivious to Slocum watching them from the second-story balcony. Slocum wished he could do something about Sheree's death, but he couldn't. They were in control and he wasn't.

He finished packing, tucking his clothing inside a blanket taken from the bed. It wasn't much of a bedroll for the trail, but it would have to do. He hefted it and started for the door when he saw the doorknob turn slowly. His hand flashed for his six-shooter.

Harriet Griffith's blond head poked through the door as it opened. "John! I'm so glad I found you. Did you hear what happened? It was awful!"

"Sheree was found dead in Thorvald's bed," he said. The startled expression on the woman's face told him a different story had been circulated.

"No, she was found dead in the bathhouse. They think a Celestial might have done it."

"That's not the story that'll be told in another few minutes," he said. "I overheard Crocker and Thorvald talking. I'm going to be blamed for it."

"What did you mean she was found in Thorvald's bed?" The woman looked at him with a coldness that chilled his soul. "What do you know about Sheree's death?"

Slocum told her. Harriet was more horrified by the truth than she had been by the notion that the woman's killer was Chinese.

"Lives mean so little to them. I've heard them talking.

When they were laying track in the mountains, they spoke of hundreds of workers dying. It meant nothing to Crocker."

"It probably did," Slocum corrected. "It means deadlines couldn't be met."

This shook Harriet. Slocum saw that he had accurately predicted the railroad magnate's reaction.

"You've got to get away from here. If Max wants you framed for the murder, it'll happen. He's got a mean streak a mile wide." Harriet smirked. "After you knocked him out like you did, he must really hate you. He thinks he's quite a pugilist."

"The grand opening has been interesting. It just didn't work out as I'd hoped," Slocum said.

Harriet stopped him. Her blue eyes turned into dazzling pools as she stared up at him. "I remember the trip down from San Francisco," she said. "And the time spent on the beach was special. You might not believe me when I say it, but you *are* different."

Slocum kissed her.

He broke off reluctantly and said, "Some parts of the Del Monte's opening have been more fun than others."

"I'm glad," Harriet said. She heaved a deep sigh and shook herself like a wet dog. "This will mean my head for certain, but I'm going to help you get away."

"Don't," he said. "You'll get in trouble with Eleanore Lexington."

"I'll be in hot water with everyone if we're caught." She smiled brightly. "So don't get caught. Come on!"

She took him by the hand and led him to the door. She looked both ways in the hall before pulling him after her. She started toward the back servant's stairway. Appearing like magic was a Celestial. He held the mark of his profession in his steady right hand. Slocum pushed Harriet to one side just as the tong killer drew the hatchet back to throw it.

His Colt spat two slugs. Both caught the Chinese in the chest and knocked him back down the stairs. From the commotion below, Slocum knew they couldn't retreat that way.

He looked around and saw another set of stairs leading to the roof. He ran for them. Harriet followed. He tried to push her away.

"I'm with you in this. Please, John."

He wanted to explain to her that she wouldn't be in any danger if she left now. If Crocker—or the tong—caught her with him, she was dead.

The pounding of feet coming up the main staircase from the lobby decided Slocum. He pulled Harriet into the small alcove with him.

"He's impersonating the assistant police commissioner. Mr. Thorvald thinks he might have killed Leonard back in San Francisco. We're supposed to take him alive and question him," the lead man said to the others. Slocum saw the sawed-off shotguns the men sported. Any mistake using those and men would die in bloody ribbons.

He took the stairs to the roof three at a time. Harriet followed more slowly, hampered by her skirts.

"If it comes down to it, I kidnapped you and you're my hostage," Slocum said.

"I've never been anyone's hostage before. Will I enjoy it?" Harriet asked.

He glared at her. She treated this as a joke. He knew how deadly a game they were playing. He was sure of his target on the tong assassin's chest. Another man had died as a result of his marksmanship. The Del Monte Hotel opening had turned into a bloodbath.

The pitched roof extended in both directions, with occasional interruptions for attic windows. Slocum ran to one and peered inside. The room seemed empty. The hotel hadn't existed long enough to accumulate the debris that always ended up in attics.

"In here," he said. "They won't be able to see us from the lawn."

Harriet stared down at the people almost three stories below. She wobbled with vertigo. Slocum grabbed her and pulled her back from the edge of the roof.

"Thank you. I didn't know I had a fear of heights."

He strained to get the window open. It wasn't locked; it had never been opened. When paint ripped off the frame he realized it had been painted shut accidentally. Slocum pushed the blond into the attic and followed quickly. His keen ears heard the pounding of feet up the stairs to the roof. He hadn't bothered to check to see if they had left any incriminating marks showing their escape route. There hadn't been time to do anything but run like hell.

"They're out here," came the gruff voice. "I feel it in my bones. Mr. Crocker's offering a fifty-dollar reward."

Slocum almost laughed at that. Fifty dollars? Joshua Beaumont's greenback was a fifty. What kind of reward for a mad-dog killer was fifty dollars?

"And Mr. Thorvald's offered another hundred," shouted another.

"You're popular," Harriet whispered.

Slocum struggled to lower the window without drawing attention to himself. He couldn't get the balky window closed. With so many men roaming the roof hunting for him, he knew it was only a matter of time before they found the open window and followed. He didn't want to shoot it out with them.

They carried shotguns, and all he had was a six-shooter

with two cylinders emptied. He would definitely lose any such shoot-out.

"Here," Harriet called. "I've found the door back into the hotel. There's a short corridor and another staircase going down. We can get into the lobby and . . ."

Her voice trailed off. As Slocum looked past her, he saw why. Thorvald and another man with a Winchester rifle carried at port arms were cautiously coming up the stairs. They cut off any escape.

Slocum considered his chances of shooting Thorvald and his bodyguard from ambush. Those hopes were dashed when he heard others on the stairs behind them.

Slocum was caught between the men on the roof and Thorvald's squad of cutthroats.

13

"We're caught!" Harriet Griffith's hand flew to her mouth. "There's no way we can get away!"

Slocum knew that it was suicide going back onto the roof. The men there would open up with their shotguns. He had no chance against that much firepower. He didn't have any better chance against Max Thorvald. The man had blood in his eye. He would not rest until Slocum was buried next to Sheree in an unmarked grave somewhere along Pebble Beach.

Slocum ignored Harriet's cries. He looked around the small attic. Boxes had been stored here, but the usual clutter was absent. It took him several seconds to realize something else was missing. The walls had been partially boarded, plastered, and painted. In other places bare studs showed where workmen had stopped to finish more important sections of the Del Monte Hotel.

"Go to the window," Slocum ordered the woman. "Look out and scream for all you're worth. I want them to all come rushing in. Stir them up as much as you can."

"You can't shoot them all, John. There are too many for that."

"Do it. And think up a good story explaining why you're up here. Do it *now*!"

Harriet did as she was told. She rushed to the window

and began shouting so loud Slocum wanted to plug his ears. He didn't. He had scant time to pry loose a poorly nailed wallboard and slip between the narrow studs. Holding the wallboard in front of him was painful. He felt his fingers beginning to bleed from the rough edges. His shoulders cramped quickly, and he felt the wall behind him beginning to give way as he pressed backward.

The tumult in the attic was everything he could have wanted. Thorvald came running in from the stairs. Two men with shotguns poked in through the window. Slocum pressed his eye to a nail hole and got a limited view of what was going on.

He had hoped the men would open fire on each other. Thorvald's bellows alerted the men on the roof. They lowered their scatterguns and climbed into the attic. Harriet kept shouting. More from the roof came in until the room was packed with armed and angry men.

"Where is that bastard?" growled Thorvald. "I want his hide nailed to the outhouse door."

"He kidnapped me!" Harriet's breathless explanation caused momentary silence to fall. Then they all tried questioning her at once.

Slocum forced himself to relax in his cramped space. He saw one or two of the men poking around in the boxes strewn throughout the small attic. No one thought to look behind the partly finished walls. For that he was glad. If anyone had fired, a dozen men might have died. Slocum wasn't under any illusion that he would have escaped alive from such a deadly brawl.

"He kidnapped me and left me and he saw you and he went running across the roof and . . ." Harriet chattered on, but no one listened. Thorvald was too busy swearing at his bad luck in missing Slocum. The others eventually saw there was nothing to be gained standing in the suffocatingly hot attic. They retreated through the window and tromped around on the roof vainly hunting for their quarry.

Thorvald finally grabbed Harriet and shook her so hard her teeth rattled. Slocum saw the startled look on the blond's face. She stopped talking and stared at the shipping magnate.

"Where'd the son of a bitch go?"

"Out," she stammered. "He went down a drainpipe and across the lawn. I don't know where he went after that."

"We have him then, Max," a man out of Slocum's field of vision said. "We got the whole damned hotel surrounded. A mosquito couldn't get past us."

"Then let's go pull him in. Swat him. I want him bad," Thorvald said. He shoved Harriet into a pile of boxes and said, "I don't want to see you around here again, whore. I'll do things to you that I wouldn't do to a dog."

She pushed herself to a sitting position and glared at him. "Since you fuck dogs, I can't imagine what you have in mind for a lady," she said in a cold, level tone that infuriated Thorvald.

He started for her. The man with him grabbed his arm and pulled him back. "Not now, Max. We got to get this Slocum fellow."

"You clear out, you hear?" Thorvald said to Harriet. With that he swung around and stormed off. Slocum heard the heavy boot steps echoing down the stairs. He waited several seconds after the last click died out before pushing away the wallboard.

"John, you're hurt!" Harriet cried. "Your fingers are bleeding."

"I cut them on the edge of the paneling," he said. "But we're both alive. You shouldn't have baited Thorvald. He's one mean hombre."

"I couldn't let him get away with saying things like that.

I'm going to tell Eleanore. She may not have his money, but she might equal him in power."

Slocum didn't dispute this. If anyone could bring Max Thorvald to bay, it was Eleanore Lexington.

"Was the man with Thorvald telling the truth?" he asked. "Do they have the hotel cordoned off?"

Harriet looked out the window. Along the roof three men with shotguns were patrolling. Across the lawn, partially hidden in the bushes, she saw a half-dozen other men armed with rifles. She turned and faced Slocum with the bad news.

"It looks as if he was right. I don't see how a puff of smoke could get past them, much less a man."

Slocum said nothing. Given the time, he could get past them. He knew it. He had spent too much of his life trailing others—and being trailed by the best. He had learned tricks these city gunmen had never even heard about. Getting away in bright daylight wasn't possible, though. He had to survive until midnight or later to have the best chance. By two or three in the morning, the sentries would be tired and their alertness would fade.

He could walk past them and they'd never know it. But that was at least a dozen hours in the future.

"You can stay here," Harriet said. "No one is going to search for you where so many have been."

"Thorvald will be back. He'll tear the hotel apart when he discovers I haven't been nabbed by the men out on the lawn." Slocum sat on a box, fingering the Colt Navy. When he saw he had gotten blood on the metal, he stopped and wiped it off.

Harriet silently tended his minor wounds. Slocum didn't even feel the sting as she pulled out tiny splinters. There had to be somewhere to hide until darkness became his ally.

"Eleanore," he said. "You were going to talk with her. Would she help me?"

"For a price, Eleanore would sell herself to the devil," Harriet said. "She's not stupid. She wouldn't cross Crocker or Stanford or any of the Pacific Improvement Company directors. But Thorvald? She doesn't much like him. I don't think Crocker does, either."

"I overheard them earlier," Slocum said. "You're right. Crocker treats Thorvald like a buffoon." He didn't add that Thorvald was still dangerous.

Slocum put his ear against the wall and listened hard. He heard nothing but the settling of the hotel timbers and the distant rattle of servants working in the kitchen three stories below. He went to the head of the stairs Thorvald had used and peered down. No one was in sight.

"Will Eleanore help us?" he asked.

Harriet shrugged. "I have no idea. If it suits her, she will. I can't see her doing anything to jeopardize her position with Crocker. She relies heavily on him and the Southern Pacific Railroad for her revenue."

"I can imagine," Slocum said dryly.

They went down the stairs. He clutched his six-shooter tightly, ready for anything. The tide of the search for him had ebbed. Wherever it was that Thorvald and the others were seeking him, it wasn't inside the Del Monte Hotel. They reached the first floor and stopped for a second.

Harriet put a hand against his chest. "Wait here in the stairwell. I'll go see if I can find Eleanore."

Slocum nodded. He didn't cotton to the notion of waiting long. He was too exposed. The first servant using the back stairs would find him. Having a Celestial stumble onto him might be as deadly as being turned over to Thorvald.

He waited restlessly for almost ten minutes before Harriet returned. The blonde stood in the corridor and motioned to him. He hesitated. He had no reason to believe she would betray him to Thorvald. In the attic she had been given a golden opportunity if she wanted to curry favor with the shipping magnate. Still, he left the relative safety of the stairwell with the feeling of treachery crushing down on him from all directions.

"Eleanore is in her room. She wants to talk to you. From what she said, she wants to help."

"What's her price?"

Harriet shook her head. Slocum saw the blond hair come out from under the clever clips holding it in place. A golden strand spun across her forehead and she brushed it away. Slocum found the gesture delightful. He wished he had time to pursue it by removing her other hair clips so she could let down her hair all the way.

Slocum ducked into Eleanore Lexington's room. It was much as he remembered it from the earlier visits. The San Francisco madam sat at a small Queen Anne–style writing desk.

"There," Eleanore Lexington said, pointing to chairs pulled near the desk. "You're safe here." She cleared her throat. A look of distaste crossed her face as she added, "For the time being, you are safe. Mr. Crocker is becoming increasingly distraught because of Max Thorvald—and you, sir."

"What will it cost for you to hide me until tonight?" Slocum asked. He had no reason to prolong this. He felt as if he were a bug being studied and didn't enjoy it.

"I appreciate your bluntness, Mr. Slocum. Some things, however, carry no price."

"You're going to turn me in to Thorvald?"

"Hardly. Harriet and I share your distaste for the man. He is quite boorish. I also happen to have a score to settle with him on a matter dating back several years."

"Are they likely to search your room?" Slocum looked around.

"That is doubtful. On the other hand, I do not wish you to stay here, Mr. Slocum. Personal reasons, as well as business, compel me to leave. I have arranged a carriage to take you away from the Del Monte Hotel and into Monterey. From there you can get horses and return to San Francisco."

"Why would I want to go back to San Francisco?" Slocum asked. Something in the way the woman spoke told him she did have a price for getting him away from the hotel grounds.

"You will be carrying a parcel for me. Using you as messenger presents problems, yet this solves our mutual problems."

"Crocker would search you for it?"

"Mr. Crocker is a resourceful man with many ways of gathering information. He wants this package as much as I."

"If I act as courier you'll get me out of here?"

"Both of you," Eleanore said. "Harriet will accompany you to look after the parcel. It behooves me to see her safely away from here, also. Thorvald has been emphatic on this point. I can, as the vulgar expression goes, kill two birds with one stone."

"When do we leave?" Slocum asked. He didn't like the idea of being used to carry a package without knowing what was inside, but the burden added little to his primary task of staying alive.

"The carriage is coming around to the side entrance now. You will hide under the blankets on the floor."

"*That's* how you intend smuggling us out? Don't you think Crocker's men would look under a lumpy blanket?"

"Credit me with some sense, Mr. Slocum. There is a shallow compartment for you to hide in. Miss Griffith will ride in the carriage, leaving the hotel according to Mr. Thorvald's desire. She will ride in comfort. Your trip will be somewhat more cramped—but still bearable. I assure you."

"Have you ridden in this compartment?" he asked.

The answer surprised him. "Several times, sir. Do we have an agreement? Your arranged escape in return for carrying a small package to San Francisco?"

"Done," he said. Eleanore Lexington took a brown-paper-wrapped package the size of her hand from the writing desk and gave it to Slocum. "Do not examine the contents, sir. This is another part of the commission."

Slocum nodded in agreement. Nothing he carried for the madam could endanger him more than he already was. Tong, railroad magnate, shipping magnate, San Francisco police, they all wanted to spill his blood.

Eleanore motioned toward the door in obvious dismissal. "Do hurry. You might want to catch the train back to the city. You would be better off not relying on anything with such a dependable timetable, however. Consider finding horses in Monterey and using a more circuitous route. Meet me at my house in three days. Midnight. Do not be late, and have the package with you."

The coldness in her orders told Slocum she might be more dangerous to cross than the On Leong tong and the San Francisco Police Department combined.

"There it is, John," cried Harriet. She pointed out the window.

"Don't leave that way," Eleanore said irritably. "Use the side entrance. The guards are out looking for you elsewhere."

Slocum tucked the package under his coat, made sure

his six-shooter was ready, and then took his leave. He and Harriet ran to the side entrance. The carriage driver stood up in the box and looked around. He knew Slocum and Harriet were getting into the carriage but made no move to help them.

"He's acting as lookout for us," Harriet said under her breath. "I know him. He's absolutely loyal to Eleanore. He'd never betray us—or her."

Slocum pulled away the blanket and saw the narrow crack showing the outline of the box fitted into the carriage floor. He tugged at a tab and jerked back the lid. He took a deep breath. It would be the last time he got a lungful of fresh air for a long time.

"It's more like a coffin than anything else," Harriet said. "Oh, John, are you going to be all right?"

"If I get away from the hotel," he said. Slocum slid into the compartment. He had to bend his knees to one side and lie on his back to fit. Harriet dropped the lid onto him. He imagined her standing on it to snap it back into place.

Crushed, almost suffocated, Slocum waited for the carriage to start. When the driver snapped the reins and got the carriage moving, a new dimension of agony was added to his imprisonment. Every bump and hole in the road caused him pain along his spine. He couldn't even hang on to anything to ease the jostling.

The carriage ride from the hotel to the gate took an eternity. That eternity stretched even longer when the driver slowed and finally halted. Slocum heard every word being spoken.

"No one is supposed to leave right now," the guard called out. "Turn the carriage around and go back to the Del Monte."

"Miss Lexington has requested that one of her ladies return to San Francisco," the driver said stiffly. "Her departure has also been requested by Mr. Thorvald."

"This the blonde bitch he was frothing at the mouth about?" asked a new voice. Slocum held back a sneeze. He wanted to twitch. Every muscle screamed in silent agony from being cramped. Worst of all, his long legs were beginning to get charley horses in them from the twisted predicament he found himself in.

"She's too good-lookin' for their like, if you ask me," the new voice said.

"No one's askin' you shit, Billy Bob. Get back."

"Lemme look at her. Gawd, she's right purty. What say me and you go somewhere for a while, honey? I'd show you what it's like to be with a real man."

"You'll get your balls blowed off if Mr. Crocker hears you hittin' on one of his women," the first man cautioned.

Slocum knew that Harriet was nearing the end of her self-control. Her petite foot tapped harder and harder on the lid between him and the carriage. He tried to move into a more comfortable position and instantly regretted it.

The bottom of the hidden compartment creaked and began to give way. He knew Eleanore Lexington might have hidden here—it would support her slight weight easily. His muscular bulk taxed the nails and wood to the breaking point.

A nail popped free. Slocum almost cried out as he felt his shoulders drop an inch. The concealed wood floor was splintering under him.

"Just a quick one, sweetie," the man insisted.

"With your kind, there isn't any other kind," Harriet said coldly. She called to the driver, "Do go on. I want to get away from these barbarians."

"Barbarians? She's callin' us barbarians!"

"You don't even know what she's talkin' about, Billy Bob." A hand rapped on the side of the carriage. "Get on out of here. If you see the fellow we're hunting, let us know right away."

"Of course," the driver said insincerely.

The horse started toward the railroad station a quarter mile away, but Slocum knew they'd never make it. The wood paneling under him began cracking. The splintering noise sounded like a gunshot when it gave way suddenly and dumped him into the roadbed not fifty feet away from where the two guards stood staring at him with opened mouths.

14

The impact took John Slocum's breath away. He lay on his back and stared upward at the bright, clear blue Monterey sky for several heartbeats. Then everything came clearer. The carriage with Harriet in it had driven on. They might not even know they had lost their hidden passenger.

Even worse, the two guards had watched the carriage leave the hotel grounds and had seen their fugitive magically appear. It took them even longer to recover than it did Slocum.

He rolled and came to his feet. Lungs heaving to get air into them, he sprinted for the edge of the forest. There he stood a slim chance of getting away from the guards.

Luck rode with him this time.

They left their post and took off after him without bothering to alert any of the others hunting for him. Billy Bob and his more cautious friend shouted for him to stop. This only added speed to Slocum's rapid footsteps.

As he ran, he considered all the tricks he might try to get free. The woods were swarming with Crocker's men. Whatever he did had to be done fast or not at all. Slocum cut to his right and ran toward the Pacific Ocean. He remembered how the tong killer had died, falling over the brink of the cliff. This precipitous route might also take one of the men on his trail.

A bullet cut through the air just above his head. He dodged in the other direction and feinted back in his original direction. Two more bullets ripped through foliage and sang off into the distance. Slocum could outrun the two men; he couldn't outrace the heavy lead slugs from their Winchesters.

He didn't use his Colt. Not yet. He had to wait for a clean shot, or he would only draw unwanted attention to himself. He was still too close to the Del Monte Hotel for comfort.

"There he is, Joe. I got him now!" Billy Bob whooped like an Indian on the warpath when he spotted Slocum standing on the rocky edge of the cliff.

Slocum's arms flailed in the air. He turned and stumbled, going over the edge.

"He fell! Damnation. Does this mean we can't get the reward Mr. Crocker promised?"

"It's ours. By right, it's ours. We seen him 'fore anyone else. We ran him to ground. Let's go see where he landed. We don't want him floatin' out to sea 'fore we claim him."

Joe looked over the cliff. Slocum crouched on a rock outcropping not three feet under him. Before the guard could speak, Slocum used his pistol on the side of the man's head. Bone crushed. The man slumped, then slid slowly toward the ocean seventy feet below.

"What's a'matter, Joe? You gone crazy?" Billy Bob grabbed his friend's legs and pulled him back onto solid ground. "This ain't time to go funnin' me."

While his hands were occupied with dragging Joe upward, Billy Bob gave Slocum a good target. Slocum rose and aimed his cocked Colt Navy at the hapless guard.

"Move one muscle and you're buzzard meat," he said.

Billy Bob looked from Slocum and the cocked pistol back over his shoulder. Someone was approaching.

"What's going on?" came the angry question. "Why the bloody hell did you leave the road unguarded?"

"Tell him Joe's got a bellyache from too much liquor and came over here to puke." Slocum pointed the pistol directly between Billy Bob's eyes. From experience, Slocum knew the muzzle looked big enough to crawl into.

"Joe's sick. He's pukin' his guts over the side. We'll be back in a minute."

"You stupid asses," the man grumbled. He didn't bother coming to check Joe's condition.

"What are you going to do, mister?" Billy Bob asked. "You ain't gonna kill us, are you?"

"Why not?"

"We didn't mean you no harm. Honest!"

"You never spoke an honest word in your life," Slocum said. His mind raced. He couldn't murder the men outright, as much as he might like to. The sound of his pistol would bring a dozen armed men running.

"Tie him up."

"With what? I ain't got rope."

"Rip his shirt into strips and use that. Hands and feet. Do it now!" Slocum motioned with his pistol to show where both men might end up if Billy Bob didn't obey. The long drop convinced the guard to do as he was told.

"Tie your own feet together. If you don't do a good job, you're taking a long walk over the edge." Slocum watched as Billy Bob did a credible job of binding himself. Only then did Slocum roll the man over and tie his hands behind his back.

He gagged both of them and rolled them to the edge of the cliff. Billy Bob's eyes widened in fear as Slocum pushed Joe over. He tried to scream when Slocum shoved him after his friend. Neither fell more than five feet to a wider ledge. It took the guard only an instant to realize thrashing about would send him over to his death. He looked up at Slocum, rancor in his eyes.

Slocum took both men's rifles and walked slowly along the edge of the bluff. He didn't want to come upon any of the others looking for him without first seeing them. Reaching the road almost a mile past the tiny stand of trees, he considered what he ought to do. Harriet and the driver had gone into Monterey. They had long since arrived and might be on a train heading back to San Francisco.

He reconsidered. Eleanore Lexington had told them to get horses and take a more roundabout path back to the city. He didn't think Harriet would disobey such a direct order. But where would he find her?

On foot, he followed the road away from the Del Monte Hotel. The scattered adobe buildings that were Monterey sprang up all around him before he had gone half a mile. Only once did he have to dive into shallow ditch along the road when riders approached.

He didn't know if they were looking for him or were simply men on their way south. Slocum decided it was better to get his fancy duds dirty than to find out the hard way that they worked for Thorvald or Crocker.

One thing he did know—Crocker's men would be waiting for him at the railroad station. When he saw a livery, Slocum scouted it. He circled it twice and waited by a tree across the street until he was sure that no one else was loitering nearby. Only then did he go in. A towheaded stable boy looked up from mucking the stalls.

"What can I do for you, mister?"

Slocum gave the boy a greenback dollar to go to the station and look for Harriet. He gave the boy a note to pass along. Then he spent the next fifteen minutes looking over the eight horses the stable had for sale.

By the time he had selected two sturdy mounts, Harriet and the stable boy came in.

"John! I was so afraid for you!" the blonde cried. The boy looked nervous when she threw her arms around Slocum's neck and kissed him fervently.

Slocum pushed her away. "We've got to get out of town. Did anyone follow you?"

"I didn't see anyone. The two guards took off after you." She looked at the boy, realizing she shouldn't speak too freely in front of him.

"I got rid of them," he said, not elaborating. "Can you ride?"

"I've done some in my day," she allowed. She critically eyed the two horses he had picked from the small remuda. "This one is all right. That one isn't good for more than a week. Look at the way she lifts her right front hoof."

"That's just a bruised hoof," the stable boy said. "She got a rock under her shoe. She'll be right as rain in a day or two."

Slocum had noticed the way the horse favored her hoof. With the stable boy's appraisal of the situation, he decided on another horse. For a long haul, the horse with the bruised hoof might be fine. He didn't intend to be in the saddle more than a day or two—or however long it took to reach San Francisco and find what the mysterious numbers on Beaumont's fifty-dollar bill meant.

"Get the owner. We'll dicker on these two. The roan and the big gray." Slocum watched the boy rush off, a broad smile on his face. Slocum thought the boy would make a good liveryman one day. He had the eye and he knew how to deal with people, even as young as he was.

When the boy had gone, Slocum asked Harriet about her trip to the railroad station.

"They didn't follow. The driver let me off, did what he

could to the compartment underneath, and returned to the hotel. I thought you were a goner, John!"

"The two guards will be getting free anytime now. When they do, the whole of Monterey is going to be like an anthill with boiling water poured down it. I want to be as far away as we can get when that happens." He looked at the blond. "You can still take the train. Thorvald isn't looking for you."

"I want to stay with you. I promise not to slow you."

The owner returned with the towheaded boy. Slocum spent another ten minutes working down the price until he got both horses and tack for less than a hundred dollars. The price was steep but not too outrageous for Monterey. Harriet changed her clothing in the tackroom. In another ten they were on the trail for San Francisco.

The lovely countryside passed by without Slocum consciously seeing it. He listened for thundering hooves behind. His keen eyes watched the winding road ahead for sign of ambush. Most of all, he wondered if they should cut cross country and abandon the road. If they stayed on the path, they were likely to run into the men sent after them.

"You worry too much, John. Thorvald isn't going to send men ranging this far from the hotel."

The blonde had barely spoken when Slocum grabbed her horse's reins and tugged toward the side of the road. His nose caught the pungent scent of tobacco on the clean, clear air. As alert as he was, the armed men had spotted them.

"Stay here," Slocum ordered. "We don't know how many there are. I'll decoy them away."

"No!" Harriet protested. "We're in this together." She put her heels to her horse's flanks and raced back down the road. Slocum started to follow, then reined in. If Harriet's departure split the force against them, Slocum decided this was a plus factor. He could deal with each group better than all of them.

Three men rode hell-bent for leather down the road, kicking up a cloud of dust. One followed Harriet. The other two slowed and hunted for Slocum.

He let them find him easily.

"There!" called one to the other. "I got him in my sights!"

He quickly learned that it was more difficult making the killing shot than he thought. He fired twice at Slocum, but he shot at smoke. Slocum faded into the woods.

The next shot that rang out in the sunny Big Sur stillness took the rider from his saddle. The other man rushed to aid his fallen comrade. A second bullet ended his impetuous life. Slocum took no satisfaction in the ambush. He had been a sniper for the Confederacy during the war and had been damned good at it. A flash of sunlight reflecting off a Union officer's gold braid and the man died. Without a leader, troops fell into disarray.

Slocum's careful marksmanship had won more than one battle for the South.

He rode past the fallen men and then galloped after the third man. He overtook him and Harriet less than half a mile away. The woman was fighting off her attacker. The man laughed and made lewd overtures to her as he held her trapped against a large oak tree.

Slocum levered a new shell into the Winchester's chamber. He aimed carefully and squeezed off a round. The man's left boot heel exploded into splinters. The impact knocked him from his feet. The man wildly clawed for his side arm.

He stared down the unwavering barrel of Slocum's rifle.

"Get those boots off," Slocum ordered. "Do it or die."

The man silently obeyed.

"His pants, too," urged Harriet. "You wouldn't believe what he said he was going to do to me. He said Thorvald had promised me to every man in the hunting party."

"Take off *all* your clothes," Slocum said. "Give them to the lady. Then apologize." Slocum fired into the dirt beside the man when he balked. "The clothes, then the apology."

The man stood buck naked, his hands trying to hide his privates as he mumbled his apology to Harriet. She solemnly accepted the forced words of repentance.

"Get on back to the Del Monte Hotel and tell Thorvald all that's happened," Slocum ordered. The man looked scared, thinking Slocum was going to shoot him in the back. He took off running, howling in pain as the rocky road cut at his feet.

"He'll take a spell getting there," Slocum observed. "We've got to be on our way. This is going to make Thorvald madder than ever."

"I don't care," Harriet said primly. "That man was disgusting! You wouldn't believe what he said to me."

"Tell me later."

"I'll do better than that," she said, her blue eyes twinkling. "I'll *show* you. It might be fun!"

Slocum took the naked man's horse and found one of the others running free. With two spares, he knew they could outride any pursuit. All they had to do was switch from one to the other, letting half their mounts rest as they hurried back toward San Francisco.

After only five hours' travel, Harriet began to show signs of fatigue. "Please, John, let's rest for just a little while. I promise I won't be long. I'm not used to this. It's hard riding so far."

Slocum stretched and allowed as to how he could do with a little rest too. They found a small, clear stream and camped. He spent twenty minutes hunting and returned with a rabbit. Dressing it out and cooking it took another half hour. He buried the fire and bones from their brief lunch and then leaned back against a tree and stared up into the cloud-flecked blue sky.

"Are you a curious woman, Harriet?" he asked.

"Of course I am. I'm with you, aren't I? How could I just let you ride off and never know where you were going?"

"What's in the package Eleanore gave us?"

"I don't know," she said slowly. The blonde came over and knelt beside him. "It's not wise opening it. She said we had to deliver it to her unopened in San Francisco."

"I can't imagine what parcel she'd need to smuggle out of the Del Monte Hotel. Can you?"

"No."

Slocum pulled the small parcel from his coat pocket and turned it over, examining it more carefully. Brown twine circled the brown butcher paper. Squeezing it like a child exploring a Christmas gift, he tried to decide what lay inside.

"John, no. Eleanore wouldn't like it." Harriet tried to stop him from pulling away the twine.

He opened the package. For once Harriet Griffith was speechless.

"She wants us to smuggle sea shells to her," Slocum said. He held a handful of pink and gray shells. He wondered why she had gone to such lengths to get him and Harriet away from the hotel—and presumably into Thorvald's hands.

15

They attacked at dawn.

Slocum awakened when the horses neighed. The first sign of trouble he saw was a large man with a long scar running across his face drawing a six-shooter. Slocum almost went back to sleep thinking he was dreaming of Max Thorvald.

The horses' continued vexation and the crunch of dried twigs under heavy boots brought him fully awake. His hand flashed to his Colt. He found a target, aimed, and fired in one smooth movement. Although his slug missed its mark, it caused enough commotion to give him time to get off a second shot.

"Damn, they're waiting for us!" the huge man cried out.

Slocum got to his knees and fired a second time. This time he was dead on target. The man who had seemed to be Thorvald in his dreams died quickly, the bullet crashing through his head. Two others opened fire from the cover of low brush surrounding the clearing where he and Harriet had spent the night.

"Stay down!" Slocum shouted to her. "Don't lift your head up, or it'll get shot off."

He fired slowly and steadily to keep the men in the brush occupied while he retrieved a rifle sheathed on his saddle. His Colt Navy came up empty. He pulled a Winchester and started using it. When he had exhausted its magazine, he got another rifle. By this time the men in the brush were convinced they faced an army. He heard them crashing through the undergrowth in an attempt to escape.

"I've got to get them," he told Harriet. "If they get back to Thorvald, we'll be up to our asses in gunmen."

"John, wait. Let them go!"

He ignored her. They had gotten this far by being careful. To let the two men escape now would ruin any chance of reaching San Francisco. He took enough time to get his six-shooter reloaded and to stuff a handful of shells for the Winchester in his pocket. Then he lit out after the men.

Slocum didn't understand their persistance. It had been two days since they'd left the Del Monte Hotel. Thorvald struck him as a vindictive bastard, but keeping his men on the trail this long seemed ridiculous. No man should hate that hard.

One way of stopping it was to get to the men on his trail. Slocum had killed a fair number and put the fear of God into others. These two would end up dead in the forest of pine and cypress.

He heard them thrashing through the forest ahead. He tried to remember the lay of the land. He hadn't ridden this way: it was to the east of his track. From the way the land sloped away, he guessed the men had tethered their horses at the foot of the slope and had approached on foot. That meant he would have only one good shot before they mounted and rode off.

Throwing caution to the winds, sure that they weren't smart enough to set up an ambush. Slocum closed the distance between him and Thorvald's gunmen. He took little satisfaction in seeing how accurate he had been about the spot where they'd dismounted.

Slocum stopped and estimated distance and windage.

He took the first man out of his saddle with a single shot to the body. The second rider required three shots. Two were clean misses. The third winged the man and brought him to the ground. Never one to let wounded prey slink off, Slocum pursued until he cornered the man.

Boulders to one side and an open glen to the other, the man tried to defend himself.

"Did Thorvald send you after us?" Slocum called to the trapped man.

"He's madder'n a wet hen, Slocum."

That decided Slocum. If the man hadn't called him by name, he might have let him go. To know—and use—his name implied an intimacy that couldn't be allowed to stand. Thorvald had set his war dogs on a specific target. Slocum had to make sure they failed or Thorvald would never get the message.

Slocum skirted the boulders and climbed as quietly as he could. A few rocks slid under his boots. He paused, listening for action from his wounded prey. He heard only harsh breathing.

Then, "I'm gonna cut you down, Slocum. Mr. Thorvald said you was dangerous. You're not so good. You're filth, Slocum. I'm coming for you."

Slocum waited. The man blundered out of his protective circle of rocks. A single shot to the head finished him. Slocum considered doing the right thing and burying the men he had killed. He decided against it. Reaching San Francisco was more important.

He circled the area, making certain Thorvald hadn't sent even more men after him. The best he could tell, these three owlhoots had blundered across his trail by accident rather than by careful tracking. By the time he returned to his camp, Harriet had everything packed and the horses saddled and ready. She continued to amaze him with her versatility.

"All done?" she asked. A slight hint of distaste at what he had done lingered, but Harriet Griffith had come to appreciate his marksmanship. They were both in deep trouble—and they were both still alive.

"Thorvald is a persistent man, but he's going to run out of hired hands pretty soon," Slocum said. He checked his pistol and Winchester and climbed into the saddle. "Think we should make straight for San Francisco?"

"Not yet," Harriet said. "We're not supposed to meet with Eleanore until tonight. We can take our time. We're only about four hours' ride out of town."

Slocum headed for the coast, and they followed the beach to the north. A bit past noon he reined in and said, "Let's get some lunch. I'm starving."

"It's been a busy day," Harriet agreed. "But we don't have to eat yet. I want to walk along the beach." Her bright blue eyes met his. She added, "With you."

He understood. Once they reached the city, there might not be time for them to pursue what he could only call mutual interests. Slocum tethered the horses and made sure they were able to reach the tough grass growing along the rocky beach. He took a blanket off one and threw it over his shoulder. He knew it would come in handy later.

They walked along the shore, the water licking up against their feet. Harriet had taken off her shoes and carried them. When they found a spot sheltered from the wind and away from where the ocean crashed against the rocks and threw salty spray high into the air, they stopped. Slocum spread the blanket.

"Hurry, John. We have all the time in the world, I know, but it doesn't seem that way. I want you. Now. I want you *now*."

He hung his gunbelt and pistol up on a piece of drift-vood and stripped open his shirt. Harriet swarmed over iim. She buried her face in his chest, kissing and licking. Vhen the tonguing turned to loving bites, Slocum was eady for her.

With some difficulty he pulled down his trousers. His rection bobbed and danced in the cold air blowing off the cean. Harriet pulled him down and hiked her skirts.

She straddled his waist and wiggled her hips seduc-ively. When the dampness of her moist, hot nether lips ouched the tip of his cock, Slocum groaned.

"Feels good," he got out. She smiled wickedly and hoved herself down harder. Slocum's hard shaft plunged leep into her seething interior. And once there, it began tirring around.

Harriet's hips moved in a slow circle. Their crotches ground together and drove both their desires to the break-ng point. But this wasn't enough, not for Slocum and not or the blonde.

He reached up and ran his hands under her blouse. He ound the twin mounds of her breasts and squeezed down iard. She gasped as jolts of pleasure surged through her. 'Don't stop," she sobbed out. "I feel like I'm going to xplode inside. Don't stop!"

He didn't. He found the taut nipples on her creamy reasts and tweaked them. Holding the firm nubbins be-ween thumb and forefinger, he began rolling them in tight ittle circles. He duplicated in miniature what she did at heir hips.

The wind whistled off the ocean and salt spray drifted rom the rocks. The pounding, frothy surf sounded—or vas it the blood rushing in his own temples? Slocum didn't now or care. All that mattered was the white heat burning n his loins. His balls tightened until they were painful.

Harriet did something inside that squeezed down hard along his hidden length. This was more than Slocum could stand. He clutched her close to him, dragging her down and kissing her fervently. Harriet's hips went berserk even as Slocum spilled his seed into her hungering interior.

Together on the beach they worked out their passion. Afterward, they lay side by side, not caring about the sand sucking the heat from their bodies or the constant sprinkling from the surf working tirelessly against the coastline.

"I wish this could last forever, John," she said wistfully.

"It can't. We've got to meet with Eleanore and find out why she wanted us to fetch back sea shells." This still puzzled Slocum. The madam didn't do or say anything on a whim. If she had wanted to turn them over to Crocker or Thorvald, she could have without the elaborate ruse. There was more to this than met the eye.

Slocum was curious, but he was more interested in figuring out the cryptic numbers on Beaumont's fifty-dollar bill: 1723. It might be an address, but how many such numbers might exist in San Francisco? For Slocum to personally check would be dangerous. The On Leong tong killers were everywhere. And the spots where he might rest easy, the police would be after him. Or Thorvald. Or Crocker.

Slocum chuckled at the thought of the railroad magnate's ire at ruining his gala hotel opening. Dead bodies everywhere in Monterey. This sobered Slocum. Too many had died needlessly. And more might have to before he recovered his due.

"The sea shells don't matter. Eleanore Lexington doesn't matter," Harriet said. "Just us. *We* matter."

He held her for a few more minutes, then sat up. His chest and legs were turning numb from the cold. Making love on the beach had its drawbacks in addition to its pleasures. He should have stayed mostly dressed as Harriet had done.

"What do you really want back in San Francisco? It has something to do with Joshua, doesn't it?"

Slocum found himself telling Harriet everything. She was a good audience. She listened raptly until he had finished.

"You have no idea what the numbers mean?"

"An address, perhaps. But where? Fah Lu has the city covered like a blanket."

"The police commissioner is definitely no friend of yours either. When he talks with Mr. Crocker they'll have both your name and description."

"It's not the first time someone has wanted me for murder." He'd always had good reason for the killing he did, but sometimes the law didn't see it that way. Staying alive was more important to Slocum than the notion of due process and who had the right to do what. His Colt Navy turned some wrongs into the proper decision.

"Things are so political in San Francisco," Harriet said. "Eleanore has clout. She might be able to get them to forget about Leonard's death. Even in the police department he wasn't well liked. Fact is, some of his fellow officers might have had more reason to kill him than you did."

"Let's get on into the city. I feel exposed out here," Slocum said.

Harriet giggled and fondled him. "You *were* exposed. Do you want to be exposed again? Just once more?"

He did.

They had a late lunch and rode slowly up the coast toward the Golden Gate. He intended to cut inland from the Sutro Baths, past the Twin Peaks, and down Russian Hill to Eleanore Lexington's house.

Just before sundown he saw riders ahead.

"We've got company," he said.

"Crocker's men?"

"Or Thorvald's. They just don't give up."

"By now both of them could be back in San Francisco," Harriet pointed out. She paused and tried to look on the bright side. "These might be gents out for some other reason. Mr. Crocker might have given up and it's only coincidence we've run into these riders."

Slocum didn't think so. He turned inland sooner than he had intended, winding his way across south San Francisco and up into the old Spanish mission district. The low adobe houses looked like Monterey to him. The only way he knew they hadn't circled and ended up where they had started from was the increasing number of Celestials.

They weren't far from Chinatown, from Fah Lu's opium den near Portsmouth Square, from the tongs that sought his life.

Not for the first time Slocum felt closed in and on the run. Staying alive for the next few hours wouldn't be easy. But he'd do it. He wanted the money he and Beaumont had stolen. By all rights it was his, and no one was going to scare him off now.

16

Slocum usually had no problem waiting. Tonight he fidgeted and jumped at shadows while waiting for Eleanore Lexington to return home. He and Harriet Griffith sat inside an empty building down the street from where the San Francisco madam lived, not three blocks from the base of Russian Hill. During the war patience had been a valuable asset. Now he wondered where it had gone.

The On Leong tong. Police. Railroad men after him. Crimps. Everyone wanted him dead. And all he wanted was to retrieve his money and be on his way.

Harriet paced restlessly and did nothing to calm Slocum's case of nerves. She went to the broken window and peered through the cracked pane. "There! I think that's Eleanore's city carriage. She finally got home."

Slocum looked over the blonde's shapely shoulder and nodded in agreement. It had to be the proper carriage. He was tired of waiting for something to happen. They had arrived early in the evening and spent the time watching to be sure Eleanore Lexington wasn't setting them up for an ambush. He still hadn't figured out why the woman had given him a package of worthless sea shells to smuggle into the city. She could have turned them over to Crocker or Thorvald any of a dozen times without such an elaborate scheme.

"She's alone. I recognize the driver, too," Harriet said. "He's her usual. She's been to the Union Club."

Slocum pulled out his pocket watch and opened the case. As always, a lump formed in his throat—the watch had belonged to his brother, Robert, long dead in the war. Both watch hands pointed straight up. It was midnight and time for answers.

"We'll go in the rear entrance," he decided. "There are trees and a bougainvillaea to give us some cover."

"You still think she's trying to turn us over to Mr. Crocker?"

Slocum shook his head. He was past making guesses. He wanted to know for certain what Eleanore Lexington's game was. They left the abandoned house and got their horses, riding slowly around the block and approaching from the back.

Slocum tethered his horse and scouted along the edge of the bright red flowering bush. The heavy perfume from the bougainvillaea made his nose twitch. He held back a loud sneeze. He shoved aside part of the thorny bush and studied Eleanore's backyard. She had turned it into a miniature park. Nothing moved except the leaves, stirred by a gentle but cold breeze blowing off San Francisco Bay.

Motioning to Harriet, he slipped through the flowering bush. The blonde followed closely. He went to the back door and gingerly tried the knob. The door wasn't locked. He drew his Colt and entered, expecting an ambuscade.

"Good evening, Mr. Slocum," came the woman's voice. "I am in the drawing room. Please join me."

Every sense straining to find the trap, he walked on cat's feet into the drawing room. Eleanore Lexington sat on the edge of a chair, stirring fresh cream into a cup of coffee.

"You may sit there. Where is Harriet? Good. Come and join us too, dear."

Slocum didn't take the chair the woman indicated; he didn't like sitting with his back to a window. Instead he stood to one side of the room, where he could watch the two doors leading in and the three windows facing street and yard.

"Your trip must have been harrowing, Mr. Slocum," Eleanore said. "I apologize for that, but you knew Thorvald wanted your blood. He is not an easy man to dissuade once his mind is set on a particular course of action."

"They were all Thorvald's men?" he asked.

"I have no idea. Mr. Crocker was inveigled to add a few of his own men to the hunt. Which ones you ran afoul of I cannot say. It is of little interest to me. You and Harriet have arrived safely. That's what counts."

"How touching," Slocum said sarcastically. "Why did you give me a package of worthless sea shells?"

She showed no surprise that he had opened the parcel. "I assume you discarded the contents along your route?"

"I saw no reason to carry them. Did you want the twine or wrapping material?" he asked, suddenly thinking of hidden messages. As quickly as the thought came to mind, he discarded it. Eleanore had dozens of better ways of getting information back to San Francisco.

"Of course not. Where are your horses?"

"Out back."

Eleanore rose and placed her coffee cup on a table. She picked up a wickedly sharp knife. "Show me."

Slocum and Harriet took her out back. Slocum watched as she ran her hands over the horses' necks, then examined the bridles.

"Which ones did you get at the Monterey livery?" she asked.

"Those two. The other two we . . . found along the way," Slocum said. His curiosity ran wild now.

Eleanore examined the bridles and saddles of the two horses he had purchased in Monterey, then began digging with the sharp tip of the knife. In less than a minute she had slashed open the leather. Fumbling around inside the saddle she pulled out a long, slender package wrapped in black oilcloth.

"Thank you for bringing these to me," she said after retrieving a second package from Harriet's saddle.

"The ostler put them in the saddles?" he asked.

"Of course. Charles and I have a long-standing . . . business arrangement."

"How did you know I'd buy horses from that particular stable?" Slocum asked.

Eleanore's huge smile told him the answer. Monterey wasn't large enough to support two liveries. He didn't bother asking how Crocker's men had been diverted so he could openly purchase the horses—and saddles.

"What's in these?" Slocum asked.

"You don't want to know," Eleanore said.

"Diamonds," Harriet blurted. "Of course! Think of all the men with diamond stickpins and rings at the Del Monte Hotel's grand opening. You robbed them!"

"They won't notice anything missing," Eleanore said. "Many had glass substituted. Too much whiskey is not good for a body. It dulls the senses."

"You risked your position to rob a few men?" marveled Slocum.

"I risked nothing personally. If caught, *you* were the thief with the goods. As to the actual theft, everyone knows how treacherous whores are. How can Crocker or any of the men blame *me*?"

Slocum wasn't sure he appreciated how she shifted the

blame for her own actions. A person ought to act decisively, and if everything went to hell, take the consequences.

"It's made me very rich, Mr. Slocum," she said quietly.

"Are you going to help me find out what Beaumont meant by the numbers on the greenback?" he asked. Eleanore Lexington had no reason to aid him now that he had inadvertently delivered the stolen diamonds. She could do anything she wanted—even turn him over to the police, if she chose. His hold over her was gone with the diamonds he hadn't even know he was carrying.

"Of course. I gave my word on this point." Eleanore looked at him. "You seem surprised, sir. Did you have reason to think I wouldn't honor my deal?"

"Hard to say," Slocum admitted. "There's no point in you getting involved in such a messy scavenger hunt."

"Let me see the bill once more." Eleanore took the fifty and held it up the light. She peered at it through a magnifying lens and ran her fingers along the edge, as if testing its authenticity.

"The number is an address. Why else would he write it?" She closed her eyes as she thought about Joshua Beaumont.

"It might be a safe combination," piped up Harriet. "He might have put it into a bank."

"Not at that time of the night," Slocum said. "It must be an address, but where? There are too many people looking for me to go hunting for every 1723 in San Francisco."

"A good point. How many different routes could Joshua have taken from Portsmouth Square to the Slaughterhouse Saloon where you saw him with poor Sheree?" Eleanore opened her eyes. "I knew him well enough. For all his profligate ways, he was a man of honor and habit. Let's take my carriage and explore."

"At this time of night we'll stand out," Slocum pointed out. "Is this wise?"

"We'll do it," Eleanore said firmly. "No one disturbs me. Not even the tong. My influence reaches into many circles." She placed the diamonds in a small drawer and wrapped a shawl around her shoulders. "Let's be off. I don't want to spend all night driving up and down foggy streets. I need my beauty sleep."

Harriet whispered to Slocum as they left, "She and Ah Toy are good friends." When she saw that Slocum had no idea who Ah Toy was, she added, "She's the most successful of the Chinese madams. Nothing along Dupont Gai escapes her notice. I've even heard she can influence the tongs—and that's something no other woman can claim."

They rode in the madam's enclosed carriage to Portsmouth Square. Slocum fingered his pistol as they drove past Fah Lu's opium den. He saw several men furtively entering. The wily Celestial had not changed the location after the robbery. Such was the power of opium in San Francisco.

"Joshua always followed the same path to the Union Club," Eleanore said as they drove. "I assume he was as much a creature of habit in his other pursuits."

Slocum watched the deserted streets carefully. Tendrils of gray fog drifted along them and sent a chill up his spine. Now and again he thought he saw forms moving. He couldn't be sure, and that made him even more uneasy.

"The most direct route to the Slaughterhouse is not the way he would have picked," Eleanore went on. "That would require a trip down Dupont Gai. Rather, I think he would go more toward the Embarcadero, even if that meant a longer trip."

"There," the madam said. "Sansome Street. A good

choice for meandering when you didn't want anyone to see you after a particularly daring robbery."

Slocum pressed closer to the window in the carriage. Many of the buildings were dilapidated. Beaumont might have secreted the bag of money in a burned-out husk instead of keeping it with him. He wished he could have known about Beaumont's injury in the robbery. Following a trail of blood would have been easier than this guesswork.

"Driver!" called out Eleanore. "Down the next alley. To the right, damn you. To the right! This must be it."

"Why?" asked Slocum. The carriage veered down a narrow alleyway. He felt trapped and wondered again if the madam was leading him into a trap.

"Joshua once said his family owned a home in the area. I remember it now. He lost the house in a card game almost a year ago. I forget now to whom he lost. It is of no consequence. Let's check the street number."

"There it is!" cried Harriet. "It's 1728!"

"The number sounded familiar but I could not recall it exactly. He must not have been able to finish the number —or the blood smear didn't mark the bill properly."

Slocum knew he would have hunted throughout San Francisco for years and never found the house. It stood in disrepair, an abandoned relic of an earlier era dating back to when the Sydney Ducks ruled the city. Without the madam's knowledge of Beaumont and his past, the money would have been lost forever.

"Do you think this is really it?" asked Harriet.

"I'll find out. Wait here." Slocum got out of the carriage and scouted the area. He was too keyed up to make a lengthy job of it. He had to check out the old house and see if Beaumont had left the bag inside.

A dark smear along the front door might have been

blood. It had been a week since the robbery, and Slocum couldn't tell. The smear might be nothing more than dried paint or rust from someone's knife as they tried to jimmy the door.

He knew it wasn't rust from a jimmy when the door opened easily. It hadn't been locked.

"Be careful, John," said Harriet. He glanced back over his shoulder. Both women had stepped down from the carriage. Slocum wanted to be able to make a quick exit if the need arose. Too many people sought him for San Francisco to ever be a comfortable city again.

"Stay there," he said. Colt drawn, he entered the house. Try as he might he couldn't make out any more bloodstains on the floor. He did find what he thought to be a path through the hallway and front room where someone had disturbed the dust on the floor. The footprints appeared deep and clumsy, as if the man making them was injured. For the first time in days Slocum again dared to hope that he indeed might find the money from the robbery.

Walking carefully, he edged around the perimeter of the rooms and checked out the entire ground level before following the trail up the stairs to the second floor.

Two bedrooms were undisturbed. The third was decorated as a child's room. Slocum wondered if the room had belonged to Beaumont once. If so, it seemed natural that the fleeing, wounded man would hide a new treasure where he had once stashed his childhood ones.

Slocum looked around and chose a small toy chest. The lid opened on rusty hinges. Inside were a few toys and the skeleton of a trapped rat and nothing more. He closed the lid and kept looking. When he probed under the child's bed with the barrel of his pistol, he hit something hard.

On hands and knees, he looked under the low bed. He held in the whoop of glee when he saw the bag Beaumont had carried on the night of the robbery. He grabbed it and pulled it free.

Laying his pistol aside, he opened the bag. Stuffed inside were hundreds of greenbacks.

He had found the loot taken from Fah Lu's opium den.

He reached for his six-shooter when he heard a creaking in the hall outside the bedroom. The cocking of a pistol echoed loudly throughout the abandoned house.

"Don't touch your firearm, Mr. Slocum. I would hate to kill you after all we've been through," came the calm words. An equally calm hand held the derringer aimed squarely at his chest.

17

"I am a very good shot, Mr. Slocum. I have killed several men with it, if you were thinking about trying my mettle." Eleanore Lexington held the derringer expertly. The lack of tremor in her hand made Slocum believe she spoke the truth.

"You're stealing the money?"

"Of course. Why else would I ever help a ruffian like you recover it? Joshua Beaumont was a ne'er-do-well and a rake. He was also my lover at one time. For all I put up with him over the years, I deserve the money."

"It was stolen from Fah Lu. If the tong finds you have it . . ." Slocum was playing for time, estimating his chances against her. They didn't look good. The madam held the royal flush in this hand and knew it.

"They'll never know, sir. You won't tell them."

Staring down the barrel of the .32-caliber derringer made Slocum want to take the chance. Eleanore might not kill him if she could walk away with the money, but he didn't want to press his luck. He was lucky she hadn't tried backshooting him.

"I'm sorry, Mr. Slocum. You are a charming enough man, but you realize my position in this. I can't let you live."

Slocum dived flat onto the floor as the woman's finger

squeezed back on the trigger. The lead slug tore through the shirt on his back. He fumbled for his pistol, coming to a sitting position with it.

Eleanore had not missed because he moved or from poor marksmanship. Harriet Griffith had grabbed her wrist and jerked the pistol out of alignment with Slocum's body.

"Stop," he ordered Harriet. He cocked his pistol and aimed it directly at the madam. "The shoe's on the other foot now."

"You wouldn't kill a woman, Mr. Slocum," Eleanore Lexington said with her cool assurance. "You're too much a gentleman for that."

"Don't count on it." He didn't know if he would pull the trigger or not. She had tried to gun him down in cold blood. He didn't take kindly to that, whether done by man or woman.

"Have you ever killed a woman before?" asked Eleanore, still probing for a weakness. She blanched when she saw the expression on his face. She wasn't able to read his thoughts—and didn't want to.

Memories of riding with Quantrill's Raiders rushed back to haunt him. With the others, Slocum had committed atrocities that still kept him awake nights with cold sweats. Killing innocent women and children had been the least of what Bloody Bill Anderson and the rest—including him—had done in Kansas. It had been called war. He had done it for patriotic reasons.

He had still done it.

"Step away from her, Harriet." He didn't know what to do. The way Eleanore Lexington glared at her employee, Slocum knew Harriet's life wasn't worth a tinker's damn.

"I'm sorry, Eleanore," Harriet said, pleading. "I couldn't let you do this."

"For him? You're giving up everything I offered you for

him? I thought better of you." The madam stood with her arms tightly crossed. She was the picture of towering anger.

Harriet looked at Slocum for support. He didn't give it to her. She had made her own decision. She had to learn to live with it.

"There's not much I can do with you, is there?" Slocum asked, his voice colder than the San Francisco fog. "If I leave you alone, you'll tell the police or Crocker or the tong where I am."

"Of course. I see no reason in denying it."

"There's nothing I can do to put you in a tight fix," Slocum said, thinking out loud now. "No one will believe you stole the diamonds down at the Del Monte Hotel's grand opening. Unless I miss my guess, you've been doing things like this for years."

"I have connections. You won't walk away from San Francisco, Mr. Slocum."

"I should kill you."

"Go ahead." The madam glared at him.

"John, wait. Don't do it. Please." Harriet begged for leniency for her former employer.

"What do you care for me?" demanded Eleanore. "You betrayed me to *him*."

"I kept you from killing him! I couldn't let you do that. There's not that much money in the bag. You have more than he'll ever see in a lifetime. Why did you do it, Eleanore?"

"There's never enough money," explained Slocum. He understood perfectly what motivated Eleanore Lexington. "The more you have, the more you need."

Harriet said nothing. She shrank back against the far wall and waited to see if Slocum would kill the other woman.

"Tie her up," he ordered. "It'll take hours for her to get free. That should give us enough time to catch the train for Oakland and be over the Coast Range before she can track us down."

Harriet silently bound and gagged Eleanore. She stepped back and stared at the older woman. "I always thought you were a decent person," she said in a choked voice. "You didn't have to try to kill him. You didn't!"

Slocum picked up Beaumont's money bag, grabbed Harriet by the arm, and almost dragged her down the stairs.

"We can't let the driver know where we're going. This might get dangerous."

"John, don't leave me behind. Let me go with you. She'll kill me. Worse! She will sell me into slavery along the coast. I couldn't stand that. I couldn't!"

"First we deal with the driver. Then we worry about which way you go from here."

Slocum pointed out a spot for Harriet to stand. She waved to the carriage driver. When the man stepped down from the box, Slocum slugged him with his pistol. He checked the precision Colt Navy to be sure he hadn't jolted the cylinder out of alignment. Happy with its condition and that of the unconscious driver, he dragged the man around and put him in the rear of the carriage.

"Let's go," he said, climbing into the driver's box with the money bag in tow.

"Where, John? We can't go to the railroad station. She'll have Crocker's men waiting for us."

"I know. I think she does too. But she can't know if I was bluffing. I'll drive you to the Tiburon ferry. You can take it north and from there head on up into Oregon."

"What about you? I don't want to leave you."

Her plaintive protest moved him. Eleanore Lexington

would not rest until she killed Harriet. The madam couldn't have her going around with the knowledge she had stumbled across. To let it slip to a few of her customers that their valuables were missing as a result of Eleanore's thievery would end her days as a madam. Few of the powerful men she dealt with daily would have any qualms about killing the madam out of hand.

"I'll drop you off, get the horses, and be at the ferry before it leaves at dawn. I don't think she'll be stirring before then—and I'll make sure the driver's in no condition to stop us."

Harriet nodded. She rode in silence to the pier where the ferry left. Slocum had less than an hour to return to Eleanore Lexington's Russian Hill home and fetch the horses.

"John?" she asked. "Could you leave me a few of the greenbacks? I don't need much."

"Here. Buy passage for two—and four horses."

She stared at him, her blue eyes wide and dry. "You won't be back, will you? I'm on my own."

"Get on the ferry and leave if I'm not back," he said.

"Good-bye, John." She stood on tiptoe and kissed him.

He drove the carriage with the still unconscious driver back to Eleanore's house. There he securely tied the driver and left him in the carriage house to the side. When he mounted his horse, he sat for several minutes, thinking hard.

He could ride due south. No one expected him to head back to Monterey. The country was wild and beautiful, and he could lose himself quickly in it.

Or he could return to the ferry and take Harriet with him to Oregon.

Slocum made his decision. He swung the horse around and took off at a gallop. He had wasted enough time. The first fingers of dawn lightened the eastern sky.

He arrived at the Tiburon ferry minutes before it sailed across the Golden Gate.

"John!" Harriet Griffith cried. "You came back for me!"

"Why not? You're the best thing that's happened to me since I got to San Francisco."

For a few minutes they watched the city recede. Then Slocum went to the bow of the ferry and watched the redwoods grow in size as they approached Marin. A day or a week and he would be away from Thorvald and Crocker and Fah Lu's tong killers.

And he'd be with a lovely woman—and a bag filled with money.